Ashira's World

The
Queen of Heaven
Returns

by

Alicia Nunn

African Anthem

Let us all unite and celebrate
together
The victories won for our
liberation
Let us DEDICATE ourselves to rise
together
To defend our liberty and unity
O Sons and Daughters of Africa
Flesh of the Sun and Flesh of the
Sky
Let us make Africa the Tree of Life
Let us all unite and sing together
To uphold the bonds that frame our
DESTINY
Let us DEDICATE ourselves to fight
together

For lasting peace and justice on
earth
O Sons and Daughters of Africa
Flesh of the Sun and Flesh of the
Sky
Let us make Africa the Tree of Life
Let us all unite and toil together
To give the best we have to Africa
The cradle of mankind and fount of
culture
Our pride and hope at break of
dawn.
O Sons and Daughters of Africa
Flesh of the Sun and Flesh of the
Sky
Let us make Africa the Tree of
Life.

Foreword

This book is inspired by the lives of youth in Gary, Indiana who survived daily trauma. Some of them were abused, raped, neglected, and abandoned.

Many of them did not have the basic needs of a clean, safe home and nurturing parents to help them grow and prosper. Yet, somehow, they found the strength and courage to come to school every day and fight for their existence.

Often, they fought the people who cared about them most, school staff. But they needed to fight.

This story is about what many of did when they were given unconditional love. They looked deep within, found their true identity and the power to transcend what seemed like insurmountable obstacles.

Acknowledgements

I could not have written Ashira without the guidance of my writing mentor, Ben Clement. His encouragement, support and guidance helped me unleash my inherent writing talent that was lying dormant inside me for years waiting to be awakened. Thank you, Ben, for seeing the writer in me when I did not see it in myself.

Thank you to my children, Joshua and Kaylyn, who inspire me every day. They are two enlightened human beings whom I was graced to bring into this world and nurture into their destiny. You amaze me, Joshua and Kaylyn.

Thank you to my parents, Hermon and Lucille, who allowed me to return home at the age of 45 when I sacrificed all my material possessions in pursuit of my dreams. Without the burden of bills and other responsibilities, I was free to write. Thank you, Hermon and Lucille. You taught me the importance of service to humanity.

Thank you, ARISE Youth. You inspired me to unleash my creativity just by being in the presence of your amazing talent.

Thank you to all of the African Goddesses, Queens, and Warriors who inspired the creation of Ashira. The many strong, amazing women like myself who have overcome abuse in its many forms. You are Ashira.

Thank you, Brother Jerome Pennington from Trinity United Church of Christ in Gary, Indiana. You sat in the pew directly behind me and I felt protected and supported by a man who wanted nothing from me as I took this journey. That meant the world to me when I was finally getting over my daddy issues.

Thank you to all the men who empower women. We need each other. We are each other. Dominance, whether male or female, creates imbalance.

Thank you, ancestors, my grandmothers, Katherine and Lola; Zora Neal Hurston, Ida B. Wells, Winnie Mandela, Harriet Tubman, the African Queens, Oya, Yemoja, Osun, Esu, Mami Wata, Asherah, and Olodumare for guiding and protecting me on this journey. You revealed my true identity.

Jeremiah 17:2

Even their children remember their altars and Asherah poles, by the green trees, on the high hills.

Jeremiah 44:17

Instead, we will do everything we said: We will burn incense to the queen of heaven and offer drink offerings to her, just as we, our fathers, our kings, and our officials did in the cities of Judah and in the streets of Jerusalem. At that time, we had plenty of food and good things, and we saw no disaster.

Love Hurts?

It's a beautiful morning, think to myself as I sit at the breakfast nook in my kitchen sipping a warm, soothing cup of ginger tea.

The bright sun rays radiate through the kitchen window illuminating the white walls and bright yellow sheer drapes that cover the arched windows. I can hear the birds chirping a lullaby in the courtyard.

I love my kitchen; it's my favorite room in this huge mansion.

The kitchen brings back memories of happy times before my family moved to Englewood. It's 7 a.m. and I finished teaching my morning Hot Yoga class in the courtyard.

Yoga helps me relax and keep my body snatched. Alia has settled to her room and the other ladies have gone back to the servant quarters.

It will be another hour before the chefs prepare breakfast so it's quiet. I am wearing a heather grey cami and yoga pants. Hugging my tall thin frame with curves in all the right places.

I love hugs.

My body still wet from the Hot Yoga, I let my hair down from the bun and my tight, black coils flow freely down the small of my back. I close my eyes take a deep breath and begin my daily ritual of daydreaming.

Suddenly, Ahmed walks into the room looking wild and crazy as hell. I jump out of my skin. Chill bumps break out on my arms as I look into Ahmed's eyes and know another episode is coming. He has that blank, cold, sinister look in his eyes, as if he is the devil himself.

Terror.

My heart explodes.

Paralyzed by fear I close my eyes, holding my breath. Suddenly

Ahmed lunges at me, clenches both hands around my neck, squeezing so tightly I just know it will crack.

He pulls me violently by my neck, knocking over the barstool as my teacup crashes to the floor shattering into hundreds of tiny fragments.

I look into his eyes to snap him back to reality. He yells repeatedly with a deep, low, sinister voice, "bitch", "whore", "bitch".

I can't reach him.

I feel the breath leaving my body. Losing consciousness, I sink slowly to the floor.

I'm going to die this time.

Ahmed always says the minute he laid eyes on me; he knew he had to have me. He loves to acquire things and I am just another one of his possessions.

I was only 18 years old and a freshman in college when I first met him. His daughter, Alia, was my belly dancing instructor.

Her family came to one of our dance recitals. I caught him watching me dance, my hips swaying up and down, back and forth to the music.

Ahmed seemed entranced by the way my slender 5-feet 9-inch frame moved so gracefully to the middle eastern music. He says when I walk it seems like I am floating.

He loves to stare at me when I walk.

Ahmed says it soothes him to watch my body move as if I am dancing to a beautiful soft melody when I walk so light, soft and carefree with my long legs. Our eyes met, and I smiled at him revealing my deep dimpled high cheekbones and perfectly white teeth framed by full lips, naturally pink, painted by God.

It was love at first sight.

I stared at him with my deep, intense, black eyes, two pools of water reflecting the soul of anyone who looks into them, and I realized he was the man from my dreams.

Ahmed is 32 years older than me, but honey he was fine and wealthy just like I had wished for when I was thirteen years old growing up in the war zone called Englewood. 6 foot 2 inches tall with broad shoulders and dark brown curly hair peppered with grey, Ahmed had an air of strength and confidence that was sexy.

He had warm, inviting brown eyes, so kind and generous. You

wouldn't think he had a violent bone in his body.

He bought me Chanel, Fendi, diamonds, and treated me like a queen.

Ahmed moved to New York from Pakistan with his daughter, Alia, his parents, aunts, uncles and servants before we met. I wondered what happened to Alia's mother, but no one talked about it and I didn't ask.

I promised myself I would never go back to Englewood, so I was all alone in Manhattan. It was a miracle that I had made it here. Our family could not afford to send me to Parsons New School of Design.

No one in my family had even gone to college. When Ahmed offered to move me into their mansion I was thrilled.

I stood speechless, my mouth and eyes wide open the first time I visited the mansion. The home in Manhattan was one of the few mansions among the brownstones and was styled after the havelis in Islamabad where Ahmed's family originated.

The maize colored stone-walled mansion, bigger than anything I had ever seen, was three stories with four colonnades at the entrance and huge wooden ornate Moroccan doors with pure 24 carat gold handles.

Beautiful archways and arch shaped windows framed by stunning blue, dark pink and white marble mosaics decorated the front and side walls of the exterior, creating a breathtaking piece of artwork. In the back of the mansion was a huge courtyard with a balcony that overlooked a beautiful water fountain where the family gathered for holidays and parties.

The interior was absolutely stunning with high ceilings decorated with beautiful golden chandeliers. The foyer had a spiral hardwood mahogany staircase leading to the top floor.

I always dreamed of having a home with a spiral staircase.

I was in awe of the beautiful large, ornate furniture and huge Oriental rugs that covered the hardwood floors. The great room was decorated in rich hues of red with fresh flowers on the tables. It took my breath away.

It was exactly how I daydreamed it growing up. Every detail was exactly as I imagined, as if I had been there before. It took weeks for me to find my way around.

I discovered new rooms, nooks and crannies every day.

The mansion was fully staffed with servants, including a butler, head maid and her staff, chefs, housekeepers, and groundskeepers.

The servants had their own living quarters in the back of the mansion. They catered to my every desire which felt funny at first. I was so used to taking care of everyone in my family.

I felt much more comfortable with the servants and we became good friends. I enjoyed hanging out in their living quarters.

The sun shines brighter in midtown Manhattan.

The air smells fresh and the blue skies so vibrant and clear. Breathing in the fresh air, I take my morning walks.

People everywhere seem blissfully oblivious of the poverty that exists just blocks away as they walk their dogs or jog, while drinking Evian water and listening to classical music on their IPods with their high end Beoplay headphones.

The poverty down the street in Harlem is not their problem. So, they don't care. Exonerated by their monthly donations to charity in Africa.

Markets with fresh fruit and vegetables are everywhere. Everyone is smiling, happy, healthy and fit. Even the dogs seem happy, not like the angry Pit Bulls and Rottweilers in Englewood.

It's been ten years since Ahmed and I first met. I can't believe it's been that long. Ahmed is a devout Muslim.

I had dreams of becoming a fashion designer, but my place now is to care for my husband and home. Ahmed allows me to volunteer at the community center in Harlem where I teach African dance.

I feel like I lost myself when I married Ahmed.

My dreams are unfulfilled and that trip to Paris the summer after my senior year in high school seems a waste of time and energy. Who would have thought a girl from Englewood would travel to Paris and marry a billionaire from Pakistan?

I wake up in Ahmed's arms on the kitchen floor. He is crying and says, "I'm so sorry, Beautiful. I didn't mean it."

I can feel the vibrations of his deep voice and I'm shaking with fear. My neck is throbbing with pain as I try to wiggle myself out of his embrace.

But he won't let go.

I give in and sob loudly. Defeated. Powerless. I return his embrace, rocking him in my arms. He looks at me with those deep brown eyes, crow's feet in the corners.

He looks terrified. My fear melts into compassion. I caress his face and kiss him first gently and lovingly, then passionately.

Ahmed opens his red silk robe and pulls down my yoga pants. As he enters me, I am overwhelmed with a swarm of mixed emotions. Pain, pleasure, love, shame. I close my eyes and repeat to myself over and over again, the words of my Great-grandmother, *love is patient, love is kind.*

Ahmed falls asleep as usual and I wiggle free from his embrace, pull up my yoga pants, and walk slowly up the spiral staircase to the master bedroom.

Throbbing, I look in the bathroom mirror and see the red imprint of Ahmed's large hands around my neck, blemishing my smooth, soft milk chocolate brown skin.

I'll have to wear a scarf for the next few days.

I take off my clothes, open the glass doors and step into the shower. The warm water pulsating through the jets in the shower walls feels good on my skin, but nothing can soothe my inner turmoil.

I am so confused.

Thoughts racing, sobbing, I slowly drop to the cold marble floor. The water washes away the confusion.

I could kill Ahmed easily, I think to myself.

All I have to do is wish it. *I can't kill Ahmed. I love him, right*?

I don't get as angry as I used to. Meditation and yoga really help. If I get angry it is not pretty. I could actually kill someone with my thoughts.

Ahmed really is a good man. He can't help these episodes. Stress usually triggers them, so I try to keep him calm and relaxed.

Something must be on his mind.

I can usually sense it, but so much has been going on at the community center I haven't been paying attention to him.

I'll have to look into it.

I step out of the shower and put on my plush white terry cloth robe. I don't have time to oil my skin. I must figure out what's going on. I lay on the bed, the 1000 count Egyptian cotton sheets softly envelop my skin and I am instantly relaxed.

I close my eyes, take ten deep breaths and whisper to myself, *what's going on with Ahmed?*

I am in a small room that looks like a jail cell with a dirty mattress on the floor. A man is raping me. It is hot and the room reeks of sweat and urine.

I am a teenage girl. I lay in the fetal position on the mattress and cry feeling scared and alone. I

wake up from the trance puzzled,
with more questions than answers.

Who is this girl and what does
this have to do with Ahmed?

Who Am I?

I discovered one of my superpowers when I was fourteen years old. I was a freshman at Englewood High School. That place was a battle ground.

I dreaded going there the first day of school. The children literally acted like they had no hope or love. Fighting and cussing in the hallways, having sex behind the bleachers in the gym and smoking weed in the bathrooms.

But they were just stressed out.

Like many depressed communities, poverty took its toll

on Englewood. We lived there for only a year and I was still getting used to it, so I stayed to myself.

I would go to the library and read on lunch hour. The food in the cafeteria was disgusting, so I would wait until I got home to eat. I walked straight home after school.

There was no time for friends or afterschool activities. I had to get home, fix dinner and help my six younger brothers and sisters with their homework.

Momma was always working at the church daycare center and when she came home at 8:00 pm she was tired. She would go straight to her bedroom and we would not see her again until the next morning. That was the routine until the weekend. Then I could be a teenager.

My life was stressful. I didn't have time or patience for those crazy children at school especially that fool Tamara. We were best friends in elementary school.

All of a sudden in middle school Tamara started acting like a "mean girl". A rumor was going around that she joined a gang. Tamara wore a red Michael Jackson pleather jacket, a black baseball cap that covered her short Gerry curl, black t-shirt and black stirrup stretch pants.

She used to be such a girly-girl and now she dressed like a boy and wore black all the time. Every day Tamara passed me in the hallway, bumped into me with her shoulder and said, "move skinny-ass bitch".

I just kept walking each time, clenched my fists and held in my anger. I didn't want to fight her. She was my friend for years and I cared about her.

The last straw was when Tamara spread a rumor that I was having sex with a lot of boys at school. In Mr. Clay's Algebra I class, Tamara sat across the room mean mugging me and whispering in the ear of one of her sidekicks sitting in front of her.

The girl looked at me, turned up her nose and said, "Hoe". The entire class laughed. I got up, furious with tears burning my face, and ran out of class.

I was Mr. Clay's favorite student, so he walked out after me. "What's going on sweetheart", he asked with that soft, kind voice that gave me comfort. "Nothing", I said. "would be okay for me to walk home since it is the last class of the day?"

Halfway up the street I heard the bell ring. School was out. *Dang*, I thought to myself. I was hoping I could make it home before the rest of the children got out of school.

I started to walk a little faster and the words of my favorite singer Brandy's song *Best Friend* played in my head, *I'll be there for you when you're going through, wouldn't you be my friend. Friend you can count on me. Call me when you need me.*

I shook my head and looked down at the pebbles, newspapers and empty Pepsi cans littering the sidewalk.

I can't believe Tamara is acting like this. I can understand why because she's been through a lot, but she doesn't have to take it out on me.

"You think you better than me ugly, skinny-ass bitch", I hear Tamara yell from behind me. She runs up, pulls my long French braids so hard it feels like they're going to rip out of my scalp, pushes me to the ground, kicking me in the head, back and legs. I curled up in a ball. Tamara's sidekicks started to hit and kick me too and suddenly I hear my own voice, but I don't recognize it. *NO*!

A volcano erupted. I stood up as Tamara's sidekicks stepped back in fear and disbelief. The heat rose from my stomach to my eyes and I looked deep into Tamara's eyes.

My eyes pierced Tamara's like a laser and she immediately fell to the ground. I felt burning inside my belly, eyes and the palm of my left hand. Tamara lay on the ground shaking with terror.

I looked directly into her eyes, penetrating her soul and said firmly, "you will NOT bully me or anyone else again. You know why you act like this".

When I looked in Tamara's eyes, I knew what happened to her and what she really felt. It was scary to feel that powerful.

No one ever bullied me again at Englewood High. I'm not sure if they respected me or were just plain scared.

As I walked home, I felt drained. Like I transformed. Strange, yet very powerful.

One of my big gold hoop earrings was missing. My yellow cropped sweater with high waist acid washed jeans, torn and covered with dirt. It was one of the few new outfits Momma managed to buy me for school and now it was ruined.

Most of my clothes were old and worn out so my feelings were hurt. I had to pull myself together, so I could take care of my brothers and sisters when I got home.

That night I had a strange dream. My mother's grandmother, whom I had never met, came to me. I had seen pictures of her. She had caramel colored skin and red short curly hair. She was round and short with a beautiful bright smile.

Great-grandmother Katherine died before I was born. She said in a soft, gentle voice, "Ashira, you are a warrior goddess, your power is love. You must not harm anyone with your power".

My Great-grandmother was surrounded by a bright beautiful golden light that felt so peaceful. She had a beautiful golden crown on her head with a large ruby in the center.

She took the crown from her head and placed it gently on my head.

She looked lovingly into my eyes and whispered, "You come from a long line of African Warrior Goddesses who have been erased from history. The Earth is full of violence, greed, darkness and you are here to bring the light. Your mission is to love deeply and unconditionally. There are other goddesses on Earth who also carry the light. They will be drawn to you. Your love will awaken the light in them. Collectively the love of the goddesses will restore balance to Planet Earth so that it becomes paradise once again."

A golden ruby encrusted sword suddenly appeared in my hand and I woke up. I had no clue what Great-grandmother was talking about, but I would soon find out.

Tamara and I went to Ms. Johnson's office first thing the next morning. Ms. Johnson is the school counselor. She is nice like Mr. Clay, so Tamara could trust her.

I held her hand as we walked into Ms. Johnson's office, squeezing it gently. Tamara held her head down and looked at the floor as she clenched my hand and told Ms. Johnson her secret. She tried to be strong but broke down in the middle of her story sobbing uncontrollably, her body trembling as she released the terrible secret she had been holding for years.

Tamara's older brother had been raping her since she was nine years old. He started coming into her bedroom at night while her mother was working the midnight shift at the nursing home.

Ms. Johnson handed Tamara two Kleenex tissues from her desk, put her arms around Tamara and gently rocked her. Ms. Johnson and I were both in tears as we felt the depth of Tamara's emotional pain.

The box of Kleenex was empty by the end of the session, wiping away the pain. Tamara's body became limp as she finished her story, resting her head on Ms. Johnson's stomach.

Tamara was old enough now to fight her brother off, but she was so afraid he would molest her younger sister that she would put her in the bed with her at night to protect her. She never was able to sleep well for fear he would come into the bedroom.

Before school was over that same day, a Child Services case worker came to the school to interview Tamara. They made a visit to the home to investigate.

Tamara's mother did not believe her story and hid her son from the police. He was never arrested, and Tamara went to live with family in Gary, Indiana.   I still think of her and whenever she crosses my mind. I ask the ancestors to protect her.

Now, I am standing in my dance studio at the Harlem Children's Zone Community Center in my black leotard and Kente cloth skirt with matching head wrap.   I look around at the studio full of 5- to 13-year-old girls and realize I have not lost myself.

I am exactly where I belong. Just like Great-grandmother Katherine said in my dream, these little girls were drawn to me. They carry the light and I am here to help wake them up to their true identity. They are goddesses. I remember my mission now. I had forgotten.

Erika is a precocious six-year-old who clings to me when she comes to the center. She lives with her foster mother, three sisters and twin brothers. The children were taken from their mother when her twin brothers were born addicted to crack cocaine.

I couldn't understand how the system has no conscience. Until I was introduced to the work of Dr. John Henrik Clark and discovered the system was started by Christopher

Columbus and a bunch of criminals released from prison in Europe, sent to America by the Catholic Church to revive their failing economy.

Pumping guns and drugs in black communities has destroyed lives and families. It seems like every time blacks find a way to rise above racism, the system finds a way to drag us back down.

Slavery may have been abolished over 150 years ago, but the system always finds a way to keep us in chains.

Private prisons, the school-to-prison pipeline, charter schools, community colleges, and gentrification are the new agents of modern-day slavery.

Programming young minds to think like a slave and locking the caste system in place.

The rich get richer and the poor get poorer. Greed has no conscience and its victims have no choice but to act out their rage on each other.

Powerless.

The oppressed becomes the oppressor as if demon possessed.

Erika was severely neglected, weighing only 30 pounds at 7 years old. She had never been to school. Little Erika had been taking care of her brothers and sisters since they were born. Her mother would leave for one or two weeks at a time at the crack house or selling her body for drugs.

Enslaved by addiction. Numbing her inner turmoil.

Erika was very disruptive at school when she first came to the center three months ago. She argued with the teachers, was stubborn and had extreme mood swings; biting, kicking and punching when she didn't get her way.

Now she is behaving better and getting good grades. Dancing calms Erika. And my big bear hugs.

I spend 10 minutes sitting her in my lap and hugging her every time she comes to the center. I look deep into her eyes and tell her how wonderful she is.

One day while Erika is twirling around in the middle of the room with the other girls dancing in a circle around her, I notice a bright yellow light surrounding her.

She glides over to where I am sitting on the hardwood floor, jumps into my lap and looks up at me knowingly with a smile. "I am a goddess. I carry the light?" she questioned, reading my mind. "I could hear your thoughts".

Amazed I say, "Yes, you carry the light Little Erika", smiling at her. I tell her about Great-grandmother Katherine and surprisingly she understands.

She seems so wise for her young years. An old soul. "Never use your power to harm anyone, your power is for love", I tell her.

You took care of your brothers and sisters as a little girl. That is love. And you can use your power to understand and help people. "I will use my power for love Ms. Ashira", she said smiling and looking up at me with those big, round brown eyes.

I close my eyes and pray for the ancestors to always protect Erika.

When I get home that evening I walk into the foyer and immediately sense something is wrong. Ahmed is not home yet, but I can feel his distress.

I run up the spiral staircase to the master bedroom and lie down on the huge king size bed. *Focus,* I think to myself. I close my eyes, take ten deep breaths and go into a deep meditative state.

I see Ahmed vividly in his office on the phone yelling. He

slams the phone down and puts his head into his hands.

I can hear his thoughts.

Ahmed owns textile companies in Pakistan and the United States. One of his business partners has been kidnapping girls and forcing them to work in the factories.

Human trafficking?

I *hope Ahmed is not involved in this.* The CIA is watching Ahmed, the phones at the office and at home are wire-tapped and the Pakistan mafia is threatening to kill him.

What has Ahmed gotten into now? I have to use my powers to protect him.

I feel conflicted because my power is love, but I can't let his partner, or the CIA, hurt my husband. "What should I do Great-grandmother Katherine?" When I wake up, I glance at a bookmark in the Koran lying on the nightstand. I notice the words "Love protects" and I sense that my Great-grandmother has answered me.

My First Love

I love Ahmed, but he is not my first love. There is another man that I adored first. He was tall, handsome, strong, protective, hardworking, and invincible.

Daddy was my hero.

He earned a good salary at the steel mill. My cousins thought we were rich.

Daddy invested most of his money into family vacations, college funds for us, and the corner candy store we owned. He drove a simple, raggedy, old red Ford Taurus. The muffler made a loud noise and daddy always played Mr.

Fix-it, refusing to let a real mechanic repair the car.

I was secretly embarrassed when my father dropped me off and picked me up from school. I wanted to ride the school bus with my friends, but daddy wouldn't let me.

Our family lived in a three-bedroom flat in a safe tree-lined neighborhood in Lansing, a suburb of Chicago close to Gary, Indiana where daddy worked. All the neighbors kept their lawns green and manicured, and pretty flower gardens framed the front of each house.

You could hear the joyful sounds of children laughing, running and playing outside until the streetlights came on, and then the neighborhood became quiet as night fell.

Although space was tight, we were happy. The kitchen was bright yellow with sunflower curtains, matching placemats, and pictures of Martin Luther King and Malcolm X hanging above the large mahogany wood dinner table which takes up most of the room. We needed a table that could fit eight people.

The kitchen was the center of our family time. Momma cooked a three-course meal for breakfast and dinner every day. Usually bacon, eggs, smothered potatoes, biscuits or pancakes and fresh squeezed orange juice for breakfast; and fried chicken or meatloaf, collard greens, mashed potatoes, cornbread and sweet tea or fresh squeezed lemonade for dinner.

The aroma of good food always filled our house.

It smelled like love.

For lunch, ham or bologna and cheese on wheat bread, apple or banana, ginger snaps and grape Kool-Aid always packed the night before by momma.

After dinner I washed the dishes while my five brothers took turns mopping the floor and taking out the garbage. Daddy made it clear that girls cook, and wash dishes and boys take out the garbage.

Each night daddy helped us with our homework at the dinner table while momma retreated to her bedroom to read the Bible and prepare her Sunday school lesson. She was a Sunday school teacher, nurse and usher at church.

The living room was decorated with a brown fabric loveseat, chair and sofa with a large mahogany wooden coffee table, two matching end tables and two white, simple lamps. The windows were covered with white window blinds.

Daddy decorated the living room with no input from momma. Britannica encyclopedias, Reader's Digest, Webster's Dictionary, and photo albums filled the shelves of the large bookcase that covered one of the living room walls.

Daddy purchased the encyclopedias from a traveling salesman. He loved to shop for gadgets in Reader's Digest and from traveling salesmen. Family and school photos in white and gold frames lined the walls.

The frames and lace photo album covers were the only feminine touches from momma in the living room. Daddy would have us sit on the tan colored carpet and read from the dictionary every night before we went to bed.

My five brothers shared two white bunk beds in the largest bedroom.

Ashur and Adam the two oldest had their own bunks. Ashur, tall and thin, slept on the top bunk. Adam, short and stocky, slept on the bottom. Aaron had the top bunk of

the other bed and the youngest two
Amos and Abel shared the bottom
bunk.

I was the youngest of the six.
Momma and daddy finally got the girl
they had been praying for. I had my
own room, daddy's little princess.
It was decorated with yellow, red
and blue Wonder Woman curtains and
bed spread.

Wonder Woman was my Shero. I
wanted to be just like her. A round
Wonder Woman rug covered the hard
wood floor in front of my white twin
bed with canopy.

My parents shared the third
bedroom. A large mahogany dresser

with round framed mirror filled the small room.

Sometimes we would all pile into their Queen-size bed while momma read us a bedtime story. Momma didn't like anyone on her white eyelet bedspread, so she always pulled back the spread.

Daddy played the guitar and recited The Last Poets. The poems told the story of the Black Nationalist movement of the late 1960s. It was ironic that the group was named after a poem by the South African revolutionary poet Keorapetse Kgositsile, who believed he was in the last era of poetry before guns would take over.

Momma loved to dance. Sometimes we would dance around in the kitchen, doing pirouettes and assemblies. She never realized her dream of becoming an Alvin Ailey dancer. She met daddy, got pregnant and that was the end of that.

Momma was so beautiful and graceful. She would have been an amazing dancer.

Every Saturday we shared the household chores, while daddy paid the bills and went grocery shopping. After I finished my chores daddy would take me to dance class. He sat in the car for the entire hour and waited for me to come out.

Daddy preferred to work the midnight shift at the mill, so he could be home to take us to school in the morning, pick us up and help with homework.

School was very important to daddy.

He had a reading disability, so he dropped out and went to the military before finishing high school. He learned to read better by reading the Bible every day.

Daddy wanted to make sure his children went to college. He was a math whiz, so helping us with math was a piece of cake, but he insisted on helping us with English although most of us read better than him.

Sitting at the dinner table doing English with daddy was like walking on pins and needles as he stammered through the words running his thick, calloused index finger underneath each word as if it was a magic wand helping him make sense of what he was reading.

His fingernails, like his mint green work jacket and pants, never seemed clean. And daddy always smelled like dirt. That steel mill must have been filthy.

"Hain't we got all the fools in town on our side? And hain't that a big enough ma-mama..."

Daddy was doing well till he got to that word. "Majority in any town", Ashur offered. "I know boy", Daddy yelled. "I was just trying to help", Ashur retorted. "I'm the daddy, boy; I don't need your help".

Ashur shook his head, rolled his eyes and got up from the table. "Fine, then, I won't help you". "It's okay daddy, you're a good reader. Everyone makes mistakes." I interjected as I sat in daddy's lap, my bare feet dangling in the air.

I kissed daddy on the cheek and laid my head on his shoulder. "Thanks, my Little Princess", daddy said with a smile erasing the frown.

Every Sunday we spent most of the day in church. Sunday school started at 9:00 am. We had a routine down pat, so everyone could be ready by 8:30 am. Sharing one bathroom was tough.

I guess it helped that there were only two girls, momma and me. Sunday worship service started at noon, and then it was home for dinner and a nap, and back to church at 6:30 pm for Willing Worker's service.

One day we were sitting at the dinner table. Daddy looked like he had a lot on his mind. He was quiet, which was unusual because he usually lectured us children about life at dinner time. "Dream big and work hard", he would always say.

I knew something was different about daddy that day, but I had no idea that life was about to change forever.

As he picked up the white ceramic bowl full of fluffy mashed potatoes, a square of yellow butter sitting on top, with wrinkled forehead, daddy said, "I got laid off from work today."

Everyone looked up from stuffing their faces and staring in disbelief.

Momma got up from her chair and walked over to him at the opposite end of the table. She wrapped her arms around his neck from behind, kissed him gently on the cheek and whispered reassuringly in his ear, "Everything will be okay, honey".

Daddy was a stern man who never showed emotion. He stood up and hugged momma in tears. It was the first time I saw him cry.

The unemployment checks were one fourth of what daddy earned when

he was working. It didn't take long
for him to get behind on the bills.
He had two mortgage payments, one
for the house and a second for the
candy store.

Times were hard for everyone,
so we slowly started to lose
customers. One Saturday daddy was
sitting at the kitchen writing out
checks for the bills. He looked
stressed out as he drank a sip from
the Bud Light beer can.

Daddy was drinking more and
more since he got laid off. Before,
he would drink a beer when we had a
cookout or when his friends would
come over to play cards. Now he was

drinking two cases of beer a day. He would start drinking as soon as he woke up in the morning.

I walked by to get some water from the refrigerator and saw on the top of one of the bills in big black letters, "Foreclosure Notice".

Daddy saw me and yelled, "what you lookin at, stupid little girl?" I was heartbroken. Daddy had never yelled at me or called me a name before.

I ran to my room, lay across my bed and cried my heart out. My hero morphed into an angry jerk as his drinking increased. I didn't know him anymore.

Two years later we were living in Englewood where most of daddy's family lived. The family of nine migrated to Chicago from Mississippi when daddy was in his early twenties, so he and his brothers could work in the steel mill. They were very poor in Mississippi, so they were excited about the hope and opportunity up North.

Going from Lansing to Englewood was like going from Wall Street to Skid Row. There were stray dogs always barking and roaming the streets, loud sirens from police cars and ambulances heard all day and night.

There was never a quiet moment.

You could hear the deafening sounds of couples shouting at each other and families arguing and fighting in the streets. The ground, littered with empty Pepsi cans, drug needles, soiled diapers and old newspapers, always seemed to be parched and there was no green grass in sight, only pebbles and rocks everywhere.

The air smelled of urine and death.

Before we moved to Englewood daddy wrecked the car while driving drunk one night, so we used public transportation. I wished I had the raggedy old Ford Taurus now because riding the CTA buses was a nightmare. They were crowded and smelled like urine. Walking to and from school or to the local grocery store was terrifying.

You never knew when someone was going to start fighting or shooting and lately the police were looking for someone who was going around robbing people at gunpoint for their Jordan's.

Michael Jordan was a hero and somehow wearing his gym shoes made poor people feel like they were worth something.

We couldn't afford Jordan's.

Shots rang out during the day and night and our family huddled in the bathroom, the only part of the house where we were safe from stray bullets that penetrated walls and killed innocent people.

Englewood was a war zone.

It seemed like the sun never shined in Englewood and there were always dark skies.

The only bright spots in this dark and gloomy existence were Sunday dinner at church, block parties and dancing. Daddy stopped going to church. Deacon George would pick us up and drop us off in the crowded church van.

Every first Sunday Morning Star Baptist Church served fried chicken dinners to the congregation which was the closest thing to the dinners momma used to cook back in Lansing. Momma didn't have the time or energy to cook anymore and we didn't have the money for good food.

We ate a lot of rice, beans, ramen noodles and spaghetti, and drank water or Kool-Aid if we had sugar.

Whenever daddy was home, he would argue with momma. One day we were sitting at the kitchen table eating dinner and daddy, drunk as usual, seemed agitated.

I felt dread.

"Abraham", momma said in a low, soft voice, walking on eggshells. "Com Ed called today. The electricity will be shut off tomorrow if the bill isn't paid."

It wouldn't be the first time.

We kept a stock of candles, in case the lights got turned off.

My dad looked up with disgust and lunged at my mother. "Bitch you always nagging me, I can't take it no more." He punched her face so hard she fell out of her chair. Ashur jumped from his seat, tackled daddy and knocked him out cold. "If you ever hit my momma again, I swear I will kill your no-good ass", Ashur screamed.

He was taller and stronger than daddy now from boxing classes at the community center where he let out his stress and anger.

Later that night after daddy sobered up, I heard him in the bedroom talking to momma. "I'm sorry Patricia, baby. I didn't mean to hit you. I will never do it again."

That was the first of many black eyes for momma. She tried to hide them but I always knew. My love for my father turned slowly into hate.

He was home maybe one day a month now. He said he didn't want to fight anymore so he just stayed away. He would check on us children, and then disappear again.

It seemed like momma got pregnant every time he came home.

I didn't understand why she kept having babies. She had six more children while we lived in Englewood, including two sets of twins. We were dirt poor and daddy was abusive and never home.

She was making life harder for everyone.

I was the one taking care of the younger children. Ashur started selling drugs to help momma with the bills and before long he joined a gang and stopped coming home.

Soon Adam, Aaron, Amos and Abel followed in Ashur's footsteps. I was on my own to take care of the younger children while momma worked.

Momma retreated to her room as soon as she came home from work at Little Stars daycare center and wouldn't come out until the next morning. They had extended hours for working mothers, so momma would leave the house at 6:00 am and come back at 8:00 pm. She was always depressed and irritable, so I tried to make sure everything was taken care of at home.

My only escape was dancing.

The neighborhood children would stand around in a cypher, rapping Tupac and Biggie lyrics. I was mesmerized by the B-boys and B-girls with their baggie pants and gold chains, break dancing and pop locking to the beat.

Cyphers gave us all a moment of peace from all the fighting and gunshots. I watched the dancers intensely and practiced at home. It wasn't long before I learned to pop lock and I created my own unique style that infused the African dance I learned at the community center.

It was a hit with all the dancers, and I was the star of the cypher. I was so excited about the block party coming up Saturday, I practiced every day with anticipation.

Finally, Saturday came.

It was a hot summer night before my senior year of high school. I was dancing in the middle of the cypher right in front of my house.

Everyone was drinking and dancing in the streets at the annual

community block party. My five
older   brothers were there.

    They didn't come home anymore
so I was ecstatic that they came to
see me dance.

        "Aiyyo, I remember Marvin
        Gaye, used to sing ta me
He had me feelin like black was tha
            thing to be
And suddenly tha ghetto didn't seem
            so tough
And though we had it rough, we
    always had enough I huffed and
    puffed about my curfew and broke
            the rules
Ran with the local crew, and had a
        smoke or two

And I realize momma really paid

the price
She nearly gave her life, to raise

me right

And all I had ta give her was my

pipe dream

Of how I'd rock the mic, and make

it to tha bright screen I'm tryin

to make a dollar out of fifteen

cents

It's hard to be legit and still pay

tha rent

And in the end it seems I'm headin

for tha pen

I try and find my friends, but

they're blowin in the wind

Last night my buddy lost his whole

family

It's gonna take the man in me to
conquer this insanity
It seems tha rain'll never let up
I try to keep my head up, and
still keep from gettin wet up
You know it's funny when it rains
and pours
They got money for wars, but can't
feed the poor
They say there ain't no hope for
the youth and the truth is there
ain't no hope for tha future
And then they wonder why we crazy
I blame my mother, for turning my
brother into a crack baby
We ain't meant to survive, cause
it's a setup

And even though you're fed up

Huh, ya got to keep your head up".

The cypher rapped Tupac's lyrics, when suddenly the deafening sound of semi-automatic gun fire filled the air.

Pop! Pop! Pop!

Time stood still as everyone ran for cover. Paralyzed with shock and terror, my brother Ashur lying on the ground in a pool of blood.

Tupac's words, a prophesy.

I heard many gunshots since moving to Englewood, but never expected them to hit home.

My oldest brother was shot to death in front of me. He didn't have life insurance, so Ashur was cremated. There was no funeral.

He was a Gangster Disciples street gang member and was shot by the rival Latin Kings.

Adam, Aaron, Amos and Abel were Gangster Disciples too, so momma feared they would be killed next. To save them she sent them to Nigeria through an exchange program our church sponsored.

I changed after that day. I withdrew into a shell of anger.

Hate.

I had nightmares and woke up in cold sweats with images of my brother being shot down like a dog right in front of me.

I lost my father and brothers to Englewood. I lost myself. My voice.

I didn't talk to anyone at school.

Mute.

I never smiled. At home I talked only enough to help the children do their homework, get them ready for bed at night and get them ready for school in the morning. Even then, I mumbled softly, and no one could hear me.

I was obsessed with revenge.

I plotted how I would kill the gang bangers who shot my brother. I suffered from head and stomach aches.

I had recurring dreams of lying on the beach. Suddenly a giant wave rolled to shore, then engulfed and pulled me under. In the water were beautiful female sea creatures and one male sea creature smiling at me and calling to me. Then, I would awaken.

"Girl, did you hear about Rico?" a girl in my English class said. I shook my head. "He got shot yesterday". I felt a strange surge of relief and guilt.

I wished for justice and now Ashur's killer was dead.

That night Great-grandmother Katherine appeared in my dream. "Ashira, remember your power is love. This is not who you are. Rise up my child. Forgive."

I forgive momma, daddy and Rico.

I started using my powers to make my daydreams come true. I focused on getting out of Englewood. I imagined going to college and meeting my husband.

He would be my hero and rescue me from this nightmare I was living.

I went to my school guidance counselor, Ms. Lorde and got some books on fashion colleges.

One night when everyone was asleep, I looked in the mirror directly into my eyes and said, "I will go to Parsons New School of Design in New York. My tuition and all my living expenses will be paid".

I felt that familiar burning in my stomach and eyes and saw the yellow glow around me in the mirror. I ran to my bed, got my journal from under the mattress and wrote the words I had just spoken, then lay down and went to sleep.

That night I dreamed I was in college at Parsons. I could see my dorm room vividly.

The next morning sitting in 12th grade English class a student assistant announced over the intercom, "Ashira, report to the guidance office".

Ms. Lourde is sitting behind the desk looking over the top of her round wire framed glasses, smiling. Her office walls are covered with motivational posters.

My eyes go immediately to my favorite one by Langston Hughes, "Hold fast to dreams for if dreams die, life is a broken-winged bird that cannot fly."

"Hi Ashira", says Ms. Lorde, still flashing that Colgate smile. She is always smiling with those perfectly white teeth and deep dimples. Ms. Lorde is a classy middle-aged woman who always wears tailored pant suits.

She looks rich.

I will be rich someday.

Today she is wearing a navy blue one with a pale pink sheer blouse. "I have great news sweetheart!" She said as she handed me an entry form for a fashion design contest.

A recruiter from Parsons was in Chicago looking for talent. The winner would receive a full scholarship to Parsons, including living expenses. My dream was already coming true!

"Wow, that was fast", I whispered to myself.

"What?" Ms. Lorde asked. "Nothing", I replied. I was jumping inside with excitement, but I didn't show it. "Thank you, Ms. Lorde. I will get right on it".

That night when everyone went to sleep, I went into the bathroom and looked in the mirror, deep into my own eyes. With determination I proclaimed, "I WILL win this contest".

I felt the heat swirling in my belly and my eyes felt so hot I thought they would burst into flames. I ran to my bed, got my journal from under my mattress and wrote the same words, then I lay down and went to sleep.

I dreamed the design for the contest vividly: a canary yellow, sleeveless, spandex jump suit with red pinstripes. A bright royal blue sheer blouse with layers of ruffles on the neck and sleeves.

In the dream I was in Paris looking up in awe at the Eiffel

Tower and I was staying in a hotel that looked like a castle. I woke up from the dream and drew the design.

I went to the local fabric store on the way home from school and asked Phyllis if I could have some free remnants. My sewing teacher at school allowed me to work on the design on lunch hour and after school.

By the end of the week the design was finished.

My design was featured in a magazine in Paris and I traveled there the summer after my senior year of high school.

It opened a whole new world for me; a world that I had only seen in my dreams. Those days in Englewood seemed like a nightmare that was finally over.

One year after my brother was killed; I was standing in Paris, France. "Dreams really do come true", I thought to myself as I remembered my father's words.

"Dream big and work hard".

I gorged on croissants, French butter and cheese and drank wine for the first time. It was legal for 18-year-olds to drink alcohol in France. I felt grown up.

Valentino's haute couture show at Paris Couture Fashion Week was amazing. It was held in the Carrousel du Louvre, an underground shopping mall located near the Louvre. The French Fashion Federation ensured Fashion Week reflected the French dedication to elegance, fashion and luxury.

The Louvre Hotel was the definition of luxury.

Just underneath the huge glass pyramid at the entrance of Louvre Museum, the hotel looked like a castle from a fairytale. There was a beautiful winged statue of Athena situated inside a tranquil waterfall. The entire hotel looked like a Renoir masterpiece.

I walked through the living room with tall windows draped in white and grey paisley curtains that matched the wallpaper on one of the walls. The other walls were white with grey crown molding.

There were rich, velvet red couches and a beautiful glass table with a golden vase full of white orchids. I entered the bedroom and saw the biggest bed I had ever seen.

There were vases of orchids on the nightstands. I jumped on the king-size bed.

The mattress was firm, yet soft and the pillows were so fluffy.

This *must be heaven.*

I wore one of my original designs to opening night of Fashion Week. A black ascot, white silk button front blouse with lace collar, pleated black mini skirt and black thigh high lace up boots.

As I rode the escalator leading to the mall the large platinum letters on the wall spelled, "Carrousel du Louvre". Goose bumps broke out on my arms.

There were tall glass cases reaching to the ceiling full of beautiful art from all over the world. I loved the "Coca Cola" by Andy Warhol. There were fashion boutiques, jewelry shops and restaurants everywhere.

My head was spinning as I took it all in.

The   beautiful   golden chandeliers, the taupe color marble walls and floor and the glass cases created a breathtaking display of light.

A fashion model walked down the runway in a dress with a black bodice, dark red skirt, sheer sleeves, and long black gloves. I felt exhilarated and inspired!

My heart was racing.

The flashes of the paparazzi's cameras were blinding as they snapped photos of my idols, Naomi Campbell and Tyra Banks. I closed my eyes and daydreamed of designing evening gowns for them.

After the show I walked back to the hotel. I felt myself floating like I did when I was a little girl.

There were thousands of tourists everywhere. Tickets to Fashion Week were expensive and hard to get, but people from all around the world came just to experience the energy and excitement.

Romance filled the air as lovers walked hand-in-hand kissing.

I felt blessed as I passed by the illuminated glass pyramid at the entrance of the Louvre. Lights were everywhere, and it reminded me of the pictures of the great pyramids of Egypt that I had seen in the Black History books at Englewood High School.

I took a deep breath and felt the presence of Great-grandmother Katherine and my ancestors all around me. This was my destiny.

The Mission

It is the year 711 A.D. I am riding a white horse and wearing the golden, ruby encrusted crown and sword Great-grandmother Katherine gave me.

Riding on a white horse beside me, head and face covered by a red, draping keffiyeh and clothed in a long white thobe, is the great North African Islamic Warrior, Tariq Bin Ziyad. "We have not come here to return. Either we shall conquer and establish ourselves here or we will perish!" Tariq shouts with conviction.

A great roar arises from the army of Muslim soldiers as they raise their swords and charge towards the Spanish Goths, one of the most formidable armies of the West.

It seems the Muslim army of 12,000 is no match for the army of 100,000 Spanish soldiers, but Tariq's soldiers are moved by the power and confidence of his words.

Tariq organized his small army into four divisions and directed one of his lieutenants towards Cordova, the other towards Malaga, the third towards Granada, and we are here at the main body in Toledo, the Capital of Spain.

Paralyzed with fear from the force of Tariq's strength and speed the Goth army falls easily. Thousands of Goth soldiers along with their leader, King Roderick lie dead and the rest of the Gothic armies flee in terror.

I am Umm Hakim.

Tariq and I were once slaves together in Iberia. Tariq was freed by Musa bin Nusair, the Muslim Viceroy of Africa who appointed him general to his army. Now we fight side-by-side.

Under Tariq's leadership the Muslim army has become a formidable force. The Gothic rulers in Spain were greedy tyrants who raped women and oppressed the poor.

Many Christians and Jews migrated to Muslim Africa to escape.

One of them was Julian, the Governor of Ceuta, whose daughter, Florinda, was raped by Roderick, the Gothic King of Spain. Julian and the other migrants begged Musa to liberate their country from Roderick's tyranny.

That is how we got here at this historic moment.

Together we conquer Spain.

Tariq is humble, compassionate, and disciplined. Everyone likes him. No one challenges him.

The victory ushers in eight centuries of paradise in Spain and ends the dark, gloomy, barbaric rule of Medieval Europe.

Islam treats everyone as equal, there is no distinction of caste and creed and everyone is honored, including women.

Slaves rule side by side with royalty.

A social revolution of peace, freedom of religion, tolerance and compassion began. The captured Christian cities were treated fairly and allowed to practice their religion.

Musa and Tariq had plans to conquer the whole of Europe until they were summoned by the Caliph to present themselves at Damascus. I often wonder what the world would be like if they had been allowed to continue.

I am lying in Tariq's arms when a messenger enters our quarters in Musa's castle. "Tariq, sir, the Caliph has summoned you to Damascus."

My heart sinks because my beloved is so honorable that he will abandon me and his mission for the

Caliph. It is rumored that Musa is jealous of Tariq's success and is taking credit for his conquests, which is why the Caliph summoned them.

In tears I kiss Tariq goodbye the next morning.

"See you when you return, my Love", I say as I kiss him long and soft on the lips with my eyes closed. My heart sinks as he rides away with Musa on their white horses.

I am carrying his child.

I never see Tariq again. For several years Tariq served as governor of the Moorish dominions of

Hispania, but he was eventually replaced by Musa's son.

Tariq defended himself against accusations by Musa. He was not restored to his former position, but instead died at the Umayyad Court in Damascus.

I wake up surrounded by African goddesses. Oya, Osun, and Yemoja greet me. "Hello Ashira", they whisper in unison. "Do you know who you are?" Oya says in the most peaceful, yet strong voice.

I should be startled that these women are in my room and I don't know how they got there, but I feel safe. "I am Ashira", I reply.

"You have no idea who your ancestors are, yet they have been with you all along. You were taught that your African spiritual traditions are demonic by people who wanted to conquer you. They taught you to be passive and forgiving to strip you of your power. Tariq Bin Ziyad is your ancestor. You have been seeing the number 711 because he has been trying to get your attention. You are on Earth now to continue his mission." "You are chosen to resurrect the goddesses on Earth." Oya continues. "Male rulers have erased the goddesses from history. You received your name from Mother Goddess Asherah. She is in you and with you." Another goddess appears.

"Hello, my daughter Ashira. I am Asherah. Because I was erased from history, the world has grown cold, greedy, and violent. Women are treated as objects to be bought and sold. The Goddess must be restored to her rightful place of honor and power, for without wo men, nothing can be created. Women who carry the powerful, creative force inside them are exploited by the sex industry. Many of them have endured sexual abuse, neglect, and abandonment. Some of them are in places of influence now and you will awaken them. Some of them have come to the community center over the last 5 years. There are people in power in the United States and across the world who carry the light. You will awaken the light in them."

"How will I get in contact with them?" I ask, doubting.

"You will know", she replies. "If you ever need guidance, just ask and listen. The answer will come. We are always with you. Meditate daily on Oya, Warrior Goddess of the wind and transformation; Osun, Goddess of love and fertility;

Yemoja, Goddess of water and protection; Mami Wata, Water Goddesses of healing, nurture, and prophesy; and Asherah, Mother Goddess of Creation. You will form close connections with us. Our power will become your power."

Suddenly the goddesses are gone, and I am in the room alone. I look at the news on my iPhone for the latest updates on the human trafficking trial.

Tamara is at a press conference. She is an attorney and is fighting for reform of sexual predator laws. "96% of sex offenders never go to jail", she proclaims. "It is time for justice."

I notice a yellow glow around Tamara. "She is a goddess. She carries the light!" I squeal with excitement. The answer had already come.

I don't have to contact anyone. My army of Warrior Goddesses will come to me!

Tamara returned to Chicago and is now an attorney specializing in Child Welfare. She advocates for children who have been sexually abused.

I immediately Google her name and call her. As soon as I get off the phone with Tamara, the phone rings.

It's Malcolm.

I met Malcolm in such a strange way. He is a world-famous health and fitness guru who lives in Nigeria. He carries the light.

His holistic recipes and fitness videos are helping restore humanity to health and long life. His ancestor Mansa Musa, the richest man in history and ruler of the Mali Empire in ancient West Africa. Malcolm looks like a king. Beautiful inside and out.

He is the kindest, most compassionate person I ever met.

Malcolm has traveled all over the world and has offices in Israel, Nigeria, Ghana, New York City, Chicago, Los Angeles and Atlanta.

His empire.

Ahmed was in Pakistan for six months on business. I had a lot of time to myself, so I meditated on the goddesses for hours every day.

I kept thinking about my brother and father and I got so angry. At night the anger became loneliness as I lay in bed alone.

One day I was meditating on Osun and went into a deep trance. I see a handsome man with long black locks, dark brown skin, smooth and silky as mahogany, and a perfectly toned muscular body. His hips sway when he walks as if he is dancing. It almost seems feminine and yet he is very masculine.

Malcolm is dressed in an all-white Arab thobe. His smile reveals perfectly white teeth with a gap. He reaches his arms out to me.

I walk into his arms and he embraces me tightly. I can feel his muscles against my body, and I fit perfectly into him.

I immediately feel a warm glow as my heart nestles against his. A beautiful golden flame engulfs us.

I wake up puzzled, with a tingling sensation all over my body.

I feel changed.

Two weeks later I am in the local Barnes & Noble bookstore. "Store Closing Clearance Sale", the sign on the front door reads. I'm browsing the empty bookshelves when two books catch my glance, "Bikram Yoga" and "Mastery of Love".

I had never heard of either book but felt compelled to buy them. I went home, made myself an almond butter sandwich on whole wheat toast and sat down at the breakfast nook to read.

I wondered why I was drawn to the books as I read. I would soon find out.

"Do you know anything about Ifa?" I ask my yoga instructor as I sit in the lotus position on my pale-yellow yoga mat. "Yes", she replies. "I know a Santeria priest. He holds a drum circle in Central Park every Tuesday and Thursday. Go."

Baba is a short Trinidadian man with short skin beautiful and black as the night wearing a purple tunic and pants with gold trim and shiny black shoes.

He is 80 years old but looks 50. His eyes, deep and black look inside me.

The vibration of the drums is extremely powerful as Baba beats so majestically with his strong hands. I can feel the beat deep within my soul.

After the drum circle I introduce myself. "I know who you are. Come with me." I enter Baba's brownstone and the air is filled with the soothing smell of Eucalyptus. "It is time for you to awaken to your true identity. Your identity was stolen from you when your ancestors were brought to

America as slaves. The Transatlantic slave trade and colonization robbed your ancestors of their land and culture.

Now, you are lost and divided. Poverty-stricken. Dispersed across the world oblivious to your connection to every African on the planet.

Your DNA connects you. Your ancestors who suffered unspeakable brutality are in you and around you. They are here to fight with you for justice.

You must study the Yoruba African spiritual tradition, Ifa, to learn about who you really are.

My ancestors preserved the tradition when they were taken to Trinidad as slaves. The male rulers who forced Christianity on our people erased all memory of the powerful goddesses who brought balance to the world.

"The goddesses visited me", I interject.

Baba nods knowingly. "Oya is working with you closely now. She was assigned to you at birth."

"You will visit Nigeria for your Oya initiation. You will become more powerful than you could ever imagine. But first you will meet a man.

This man will open your heart. You are already a powerful woman, but fear is blocking your heart from fully opening. You may mistake what you feel about what happened to your brother and family for anger. But the anger masks fear."

Fear?

"You fear love", Baba reads my mind. "When your heart opens fully you will become more powerful." I feel confused. "I love my husband, so how will this man open my heart?"

"You will see. You still have a lot to learn about love." Baba replies wisely, his eyes glistening.

The next day I enter yoga class distracted by Baba's words and the room is dimly lit, so I don't notice the new instructor. "Hello, my name is Malcolm", says a deep, low, gentle voice. I look up in disbelief as I recognize the voice from my dream.

I stand paralyzed with doubt for a moment. After class I walk outside with my yoga mat under my arm, feeling dazed and confused.

Malcolm walks out after me and says, "Good Day, what is your name, Beautiful?" as he smiles revealing those white teeth and gap from my dream.

He embraces me tightly and my
body grows limp as I feel the warm
energy from his heart against mine.
Everything around us disappears and
the only thing that exists in this
moment is he and I.

I Am Mina

I'm sitting at the breakfast nook daydreaming with my eyes closed, sipping warm ginger tea from my favorite cup, when my mind slips back to childhood. It's been 10 years since I saw my family.

Sometimes I feel guilty, like I abandoned my little brothers and sisters, but I vowed to leave that life behind, and I haven't looked back. It feels like my old life is still haunting me though.

I'm more like my mother than I ever wanted. I don't think I ever saw her do anything selfish.

She always took care of everyone, except herself. She washed and ironed all of our clothes and prepared full course, homecooked meals every day. Well, before we moved to Englewood, anyway.

Momma always put tender loving care in everything she did. Like when she ironed daddy's church shirts. She paid special attention to every detail, laying the shirt across the ironing board so carefully, as if daddy was actually inside the shirt.

Momma sprayed the collar and each arm with Niagara starch, then ironed and creased them to perfection. The shirt would be so stiff that it could stand up on its own.

Momma cared for everyone at church too. She took care of the children at the day care center, taught Sunday school, served on the usher and nurse's board, and helped cook First Sunday dinner.

Momma was an amazing cook.

Her seven-up pound cake was fluffy and moist on the inside and golden brown on the outside. You could smell the aroma of real butter filling the house.

We couldn't wait to taste it.

Momma always made us sit still while the cake was in the oven, so it wouldn't sink in the middle. We would tiptoe and look inside the oven window to see if it was almost done.

She let us lick the mixing spoon and bowl, so the anticipation wouldn't kill us. Momma's seven-up cake was the favorite at church.

Smiling, I remember my mother in her church nurse uniform. She always looked so pretty in her perfectly pressed white dress and nurse's hat with white opaque tights and flawless white lace up shoes.

She was an usher on Sunday morning and a nurse on Friday nights for tarry service. Brother Charles played a tune that sounded like blues music as Ashur banged away on the drums.

"Thank you, Jesus, thank you, Jesus", the church members chanted in unison as everyone danced around.

Momma would scurry with the red blanket to the rescue of church members who "caught the holy ghost" and fell out cold in the floor.

Sister Partridge completely lost her mind when she caught the Holy Ghost every week.

She would hit people, bump her head on the wooden church pew and work her way to the altar, fall out on the plush crimson red carpet, skirt flying up revealing her white silk slip and matching granny panties.

That red carpet was the blood of Jesus washing away all her troubles, the way she rolled around on it with no self-control.

We would snicker and shake our heads, wondering why the Holy Ghost didn't tell her not to bump her head and show her panties to the whole church.

I understand better now, catching the Holy Ghost was the only therapy Sister Partridge had to cope with her cheating and beating husband. *I wonder if she's still with him*, I think to myself, shaking my head.

Momma's salmon patties were my favorite. I would stand next to her at the kitchen counter and watch her mix the canned salmon with eggs, onions, and green peppers in the big white mixing bowl. She let me shake salt and black pepper into the mixture.

Then she would roll the salmon into balls and mash them gently with the palm of her hands into perfectly round patties. She would dip them into a flour and cornmeal mixture and place them carefully onto the big, black cast iron skillet where a dollop of lard had been melting on the stovetop. Those salmon patties always tasted as good as they smelled.

Yummy.

Momma baked our birthday cakes from scratch and decorated them herself. Our parties were always special. Of course, I had to have Wonder Woman decorations for my party.

Momma made our Halloween costumes herself, too.

I remember the time she dressed me as a witch. I was 5 years old, and I felt so grown up when she put that long black wig and red lipstick on me. I had the pointy hat and long black dress, too.

I chuckle to myself just thinking about it.

Momma made us popcorn balls from scratch. Her popcorn tasted so good. She would pop it in the same pot every time, a big grey pot with green top.

I always wondered why the top didn't match the pot.

I loved to hear the sound of the kernels hitting the pot top as the pressure built up slowly at first then rapidly, then slow again as the last kernels exploded into fluffy white blossoms.

Momma would melt butter in a skillet then pour it over the popcorn and sprinkle just the right amount of salt. It tasted better than movie popcorn. I loved to crunch on the half-popped kernels.

Popcorn is still my favorite food.

Great food are my best memories from childhood.

Playing outside with our neighbors is also a fond memory. "Ms. Mary Mack, Mack, Mack. All dressed in black, black, black. With silver buttons, buttons, buttons, all down her back, back, back", Tony would sing as she and her sister Sugar turned the jump rope in perfect rhythm.

I was the Double Dutch queen.

Tony and Sugar would get tired and I was still going strong. I had so much energy. No one could keep up with me.

My mind drifts to the children at the community center. They come to the center with stress lines covering their foreheads and worry on their faces. I feel sorry that they don't get to play like we did.

Video games, computers, iPads and iPhones have replaced good old-fashioned fun. At least the girls can be children and feel free while they dance at the center.

I better get up and get ready.

I bound up the spiral staircase to my bedroom to get dressed.

It's the first day of class for the summer program, so the children come in the morning instead of the evening.

I walk through the glass doors painted with a mural of children dancing with a blue sky, white clouds and bright yellow sun in the background as if they are floating in the air.

I feel excited to meet a new group of twenty 5- to 13-year-old girls, but also sad that these children have so many struggles at such a tender age.

I feel hopeful that each of them will be transformed as they dance.

As I walk to my office, my eyes fall on Mina crouched on the floor in the corner of the room at the end of the mirrored wall wearing black leotard and pink tights.

I recognize her from the picture sent over by Child Services with her application. She is a thin, tall 13-year-old with long black hair, big, round, black eyes and caramel-colored skin. *She looks Middle Eastern*.

I ask my assistant, Pamela to line the other girls up for warm up. I walk over to Mina and reach out to her, smiling, as she looks up at me. She reaches back, and I guide her to my office. As I close the door behind us, I hear Pam begin the warm-up.

"What's wrong, honey?" Mina
looks down at the floor and doesn't
answer. I take a deep breath in.

How do I reach Mina?

Immediately I sense that I've
seen Mina before. هل تتحدث
الانجليزية, I ask in the Arabic Alia
and Ahmed taught me. "لا", she
replied.

I had a feeling she was Middle
Eastern, so I asked her if she spoke
English and she replied, "No". "
أنت آمن، ثق بي You are safe, trust
me." I reassure her.

I see a hint of a smile as I
reach out to her again and twirl her
gently. I lead her back to the rest

of the group, smile, run back to my office and close the door.

I fall onto the plush yellow leather couch in my office, weeping controllably.

When I touched Mina's hand the second time, I saw a flash of her and immediately knew why she seemed so familiar.

How did she get here? I must find out what is going on. I will look into it when I get home.

I was distracted the rest of the session. When it was finally over, I lock up the center and run to the subway, hop on the Red Line to Grand Central Station, then take the S train to Manhattan.

The ride takes 30 minutes and it feels like I will never get home. Thankfully, the trains are not that crowded. I sit shaking my leg nervously thinking about Mina.

Finally, home.

I run up the spiral staircase to the master bedroom, sit in the middle of the floor in lotus position, close my eyes and breathe. *One, two, three,* I count to myself as I breathe in and out deeply through my nose.

Take me to Mina.

I am in the room again. Two young Middle Eastern women who seem to be 19 or 20 years old are hugging me, trying to comfort me as I sob loudly. "It's okay, you'll get used to it like we did."

"You tricked me!" I scream, pushing them away. "My parents think I am a nanny. You lied to them!" My voice is trembling as my body shakes in terror and pain.

I am Mina.

Later that same night Ahmed's partner comes into the room where I was raped, grabs me by the arm and pulls me up. I try to pull away and he punches me in the face.

I fall onto the dirty mattress and he takes out a needle and sticks into my wrist. I lose consciousness.

I wake up with a dirty brown blanket wrapped around my face and body, my arms tied behind my back with a rope, lying on the floor of a van.

I am terrified.

Oya is Powerful

Mina was smuggled from Pakistan to the United States and sold to a prostitution ring in New York. She was raped and drugged every day.

During the day Mina stood in Times Square with a group of other girls wearing only body paint and thong panties, posing for photographs with tourists.

She was a favorite.

At night she was forced to have sex with high profile businessmen and politicians who traveled to New York City from every nation at upscale hotels.

One night a customer passed out from alcohol and cocaine intoxication after having sex with Mina.

His heavy, pale, hairy body lay listless on top of her.

Mina manages to wrestle her way from under him. She tiptoes to the bathroom, terrified that he will wake up, puts on the plush, white terry cloth robe, "Waldorf Astoria" embroidered with black thread on the right chest.

She runs barefoot to the back stairwell marked "Exit" in green neon. "Help me Allah", Mina prays as she runs down sixteen flights of stairs without stopping, feeling propelled.

She pushes open the steel back door leading to the alley, avoiding the goon waiting in the hotel lobby. Mina runs through the crowded streets, ignoring the tourists puzzled stares.

Blinded by tears.

Finally, she bumps into two police officers and collapses on the ground. The officers carry her to the police station nearby and call Child Services.

An Arabic speaking worker arrives, and Mina tells them her story.

Even the officers with stern faces, blue uniforms and muscular arms crossed in front of them are moved to tears by her words. "No matter how much crime we see every day, I never get used to someone hurting a child. I hope I catch that son-of-a-bitch and cut his balls off", one of the officers booms.

The case worker assigned to Mina is my friend, Katrina. She knows about my dance class and sends her. She figured I could help Mina.

It takes weeks to locate Mina's parents since she didn't have any identification. The next day I call

Katrina. Her parents have not been
found and it is feared they have
been killed.

Ahmed has been in Pakistan for
six months, so I decide to pay him
a visit.

*I can get more answers in
Pakistan.*

I try to use my powers to find
more about Ahmed's involvement, but
it's not working. Something is
blocking it.

I have grown.

Seeing the condition of Mina
and many other girls like her would
have provoked my rage years ago and
the men who captured her would die

instantly from my gaze, but I feel peace. I know that only love can fix this terrible situation.

The plane ride is long. I'm sitting next to my friend Bilal who is traveling with me. He is a Saudi Arabian from France.

I met him on the subway in Harlem. Bilal is a delightful 19-year-old, tall thin, muscular with dark short hair and dark thick eyebrows. The women love his dimpled smile.

He speaks French and Arabic with a thick Middle Eastern accent. He doesn't speak much English and I speak a little French and Arabic, but somehow, we understand each other.

I met Bilal on the subway last summer on my way to the community center in Harlem. He works as a property manager for one of the biggest real estate developers in New York. His dream is to become a rapper, so his side hustle is promoting upscale night clubs.

We have fun exploring Harlem. All the cultures there fascinate me: Nigerian, Dominican, Trinidadian, Cuban. Their brown skin looks the same and the only difference is their language.

Sometimes I sit and watch Bilal clean the apartments where young people travel from across the world to rent a room in search of the American dream, chasing riches they never find.

The morning air is always filled with aromas of bacon frying and pancakes. I don't eat pork anymore, but I breathe in the aroma, closing my eyes.

It smells so good.

I sit at the kitchen table and sip ginger tea from a white mug labeled "IKEA". All the apartments Bilal cleans have white iron beds; white duvet covers, a white floor lamp and black furniture with red decorative pillows.

As I go to the bathroom to wash my hands, I hear someone singing and playing piano through the open window.

They must be practicing for an audition, I smile to myself.

It sounds beautiful and I can feel the vibrations of the music and powerful alto voice deep inside.

Only in New York.

People of all ages sit on chairs in front of the brownstones lining the Harlem streets, talking in their native language and laughing loudly. The children playing on the sidewalk remind me of Englewood. My thoughts go back to the violence that took my brother.

Today I decide to go for a walk down 125th Street while Bilal is cleaning an apartment. I enjoy seeing people mingling and walking in the streets. It keeps the loneliness away since Ahmed has been in Pakistan so long. The air is warm and fresh, not like the smell of sewage in Times Square.

I breathe in deep and float down the street when I see Baba. "Hello beautiful Sista, how are you?" He says in a gentle voice. I smile, "I'm fine". "Yes, you are",

he replies, smiling mischievously.
He is different today.

"You will travel soon, Ashira."
Baba says pensively. "You will
receive your instructions as you
travel, and you will understand why
Bilal is with you. It is no
coincidence.
Everything is connected." Baba
says. "I'm going to my drum circle.
Come with me."

As we enter Central Park from
125th I feel a little distracted. A
group of people sit in a circle in
the middle of Central Park. My
worries melt away instantly as Baba
beats the drum with his large,

wrinkled hands, black and beautiful like onyx.

The powerful rhythm and beat vibrate my entire being and sets my heart afire.

The other drummers follow Baba's lead as the sounds of the Earth's heartbeat pierce the atmosphere enveloping the park. Everyone seems to walk and flow to the rhythm of the beat.

Harmony.

A black stretch limousine meets Bilal and me at the airport in Islamabad. We walk down the stairs of Ahmed's private Lear jet and are greeted by a tall emaciated man with pale skin, black short hair, black mustache and goatee, thick black eyebrows and eyelashes framing beady, and sunken eyes with dark circles.

He steps out of the limousine to greet us. I have never seen Ahmed's partner. His identity was always top secret. Bilal's golden-brown skin suddenly becomes pale.

"What's wrong Bilal?" I ask. "I will tell you later", he whispers.

I am wearing a black hijab and my entire body is covered in a long draping black dress with black pump heels. Black slacks underneath the dress covers me.

The scorching heat takes my breath away. I've visited Pakistan before, but I never get used to the heat.

"Salaam alaykum", Ahmed's partner greets us, shaking my hand and kissing my right cheek once, then my left cheek twice.

His cold lips and hands send chills down my spine. I almost feel afraid. "I didn't expect you to be traveling with Ashira, Bilal", he says suspiciously in Arabic. "Ahmed will not be happy".

I reassure him, "It's none of your business, but Bilal is like family".

You could hear a pin drop in the limousine on the way to Ahmed's mansion. It's so quiet and Bilal seems nervous, looking at the floor, forehead wrinkled, wringing his hands. Thank goodness Ahmed's partner sits in front with the driver.

Bilal and I share the roomy back seat.

When we arrive at the mansion Ahmed is not there. The servants get our bags out of the limousine. "Ashira, I will pick you up in two hours and take you to Ahmed. Get freshened up and eat. I will return."

Bilal is still quiet as we walk inside. The mansion looks exactly like the one in Manhattan except larger. We climb the spiral staircase lined with plush red carpet, holding tightly onto the pure gold railing as if to keep us both grounded.

Eerie.

The servants take Bilal to a room in their quarters and I go to the master bedroom. I lie on the bed, close my eyes and take ten deep breaths.

Take me to Bilal.

Something tells me it's not safe to talk in the mansion, so I use my powers to find out what Bilal wants to tell me.

"Ahmed's partner is CEO of the real estate development company I work for. He is a very bad man", I hear Bilal's thoughts. "We are not safe, Ashira. We must get out of here".

I feel Bilal's overwhelming dread.

We are safe. The goddesses are here protecting us. There is nothing to fear. Love is more powerful than Ahmed's partner.

I feel Bilal relax as I send waves of love telepathically.

Take me to the goddesses.

Oya, Osun, Yemoja and Asherah immediately gather around the bed.

I smile at Oya as she looks at me lovingly and says, "As you begin your journey, Ashira, it's important for you to know the history. There is nothing new about sex slavery. Children and women have been sold as property for many centuries. Capitalism, as it is called today has plagued our world since ancient times. The truth has been hidden and now it is being revealed. Sex slavery dates back to the Ottoman Empire. The lives of the rulers were valued as more than the poor, justifying slavery in all its forms, including sex slavery."

A map suddenly appears.

"Palestine, Land of Israel, in the past was a trade link between Europe, North Africa, Asia and India that included many cultures, religions and empires. As you can see from the map, Israel is at the center. You must travel to Palestine where this all began. There is a portal that you and Malcolm must open to bring back the power to awaken leaders across the world. First you must travel to Peru to receive power from an energy vortex in the Machu Picchu Mountains. When you arrive pray to Esu to open the portal. Meanwhile meditate on me every day before you go."

Every morning I meditate on Oya before I start my day. I develop a close connection to her.

Then, something unexplainable happens. I feel an energy vortex on top of my head opening and connecting me to a power source. The weather outside is sunny and calm, then suddenly the sky darkens, and the wind blows fiercely.

Oya is powerful!

Homecoming

I take a deep breath in and out as I step into the limousine with Ahmed's partner.

Sitting alone in the back seat, I feel the goddesses in and around me. The windows are tinted inside and outside so I can't see where I am going.

We've been driving for over an hour when the limousine stops suddenly. The driver opens my door and I step out onto a dirt road lined by wooden shacks. The stench from the sewer running through a ditch in the middle of the road is almost unbearable as I cover my nose with my hijab.

Where are we?

I follow Ahmed's partner to a nearby shack. Somehow, I am not afraid.

I walk into the front door guarded by two muscle-bound goons with automatic rifles in their crossed arms. They look straight ahead as I follow Ahmed's partner into the shack.

My heart stops as I see Ahmed and an older woman who looks like Alia sitting at a wooden table with their hands and feet tied. I run to Ahmed in tears and embrace him.

He sobs. "I'm so sorry Ashira", he whispers in my ear.

Ahmed's partner pulls me away and slams me into a chair. I look him directly in the eyes.

Be careful. You do not know who I am.

He steps back.

"It seems your husband has another wife. What will you do now?" He snorts. "You are very beautiful, perhaps I should sell you."

I proclaim calmly, but firmly, looking directly in his eyes. "I am not afraid. Why have you detained my husband?"

"Your husband thought he could rescue his first wife."

Ahmed's wife, Miriam has been held by his partner for over ten years. He raped her in front of Ahmed and kidnapped her shortly before the family moved to the United States.

Miriam has been a servant to the girls and women Ahmed's partner kidnapped and sold into sex slavery.

That explains Ahmed's episodes.

Ahmed's partner was a former servant who forced him to give up half of his company in exchange for sparing Miriam's life. Ahmed found

Miriam during his visit and was captured while attempting to rescue her.

Help me Oya.

I'm sure Ahmed's partner has plans to kill me. He has no use for me, except to control Ahmed.

"You will not get away with this", I say, looking directly into Ahmed's partner's eyes. He falls to the floor from the power of my gaze.

I look directly into the eyes of the goons who are now pointing guns at me. Their guns fall to the ground as they stand paralyzed, looking in disbelief.

The ruby encrusted sword appears in my hand and I cut the ropes and free Ahmed and Miriam. We run to the limousine.

Ahmed drives us to the mansion where we pick up Bilal, the family and servants. As we drive to the airport, I explain to Ahmed that we must travel to Englewood.

We will be safe there.

On the plane I fall into a deep sleep and Asherah appears in my dream, "Beloved, I know it must be hard to know that Ahmed has another wife, but you must persevere. In time you will understand. Here is some information that will help you with your mission."

A timeline appears in front of me dating back to 900 BC when hunter-gatherers settled in Jericho.

Patriarchs formed in 1900 BC and the fighting began.

There have been many empires that conquered Israel: Egyptian, Assyrian, Babylonian, Persian, Greek, Roman, Ottoman and many others.

The violent cycles have continued for centuries.

The Ottoman Empire is the most recent.

To restore harmony to Earth the Mother Creator energy must reunite with the Father energy.

The power is in you, Ashira. And the seed to activate this power is in your soul mate.

You will travel to Peru, Egypt, Nigeria, and finally to Israel.

Before you can continue this journey, Ashira, you must find peace with your past.

Your heart must be totally clear for the love to be strong enough. Once you are at peace, travel to Peru and Egypt. There is feminine power in each of these places.

You will find it in the Andes Mountains of Machu Picchu in Peru and the Kings Chamber of the Great Pyramid in Egypt. Then, go to Nigeria for your Oya initiation before you travel to Israel where you will meet Malcolm.

You will receive further instructions.

My thoughts are racing on the plane ride to Chicago. I haven't been home since 2007.

Memories flood my mind. I smile at thoughts of Christmas. Those were happy times. I remember the Easy Bake Oven, snow cone maker and peanut butter maker daddy bought me over the years.

He always bought useful toys. And we loved when daddy made snow cream. We would take large metal bowls outside and fill them with cold, crisp, white snow. That was back when the air was still clean. He would pour pet milk and sugar in the bowl and let it dissolve.

Yummy.

One Christmas daddy bought us all musical instruments: an acoustic guitar for me, drum set for Ashur, electric keyboard for Adam, flute for Aaron and bongos for Amos and tambourine for Abel.

We felt like the Jackson Five, harmonizing in perfect pitch, "A-B-C, easy as 1-2-3…" I was the lead singer. Even though Michael was a boy, people said I sounded just like him.

Daddy could sing and draw. He was a background singer for gospel singers like Shirley Caesar and James Cleveland when he was younger.

The steel mill sucked the life out of daddy.

The death of the steel industry put the nail in the coffin. We are a creative family, not meant to toil and grind like slaves on a plantation.

We were meant to be free.

I take a deep breath in as the limousine approaches my childhood home.

Englewood seems different now. The people are still poor and there are boarded up abandoned buildings everywhere, but I feel hope.

I knock on the door, the air floods out of my lungs as I exhale. It seems like I've been holding my breath for a lifetime. Tears fill my eyes as the door opens and I am face-to-face with my past.

I collapse into my father's arms and weep from my soul. I melt into him.

I am daddy's little girl again.

He seems so peaceful now. He was discharged from rehab a new man. While in a drunken stupor, daddy beat momma so bad that she spent weeks in the hospital.

He was sentenced to probation and rehab since he had no record. My younger siblings were placed in foster care until momma recovered.

She was court ordered to receive domestic violence group counseling.

Daddy's face glows as he smiles, telling the story of his transformation. Daddy wrote songs and drew sketches in prison. It helped him find peace.

My kind, gentle, loving father is back.

Momma looks very thin and worn from holding the family together, but there is a twinkle in her eyes as she looks adoringly at my father.

The love of her life.

Daddy teaches music to inner city youth and his songs are published on iTunes. His drawings are hanging in restaurants and businesses across Chicago.

Momma never realized her dream of being a dancer, but she seems satisfied that her family is together again.

"I been following you all these years, Ashira, and praying for the Good Lord to protect you", Momma said as she brings a beautiful Mahogany box from her bedroom, sits it on the kitchen table and opens it gently.

There were news clippings of my trip to Paris, pictures of my wedding and dozens of unopened letters tied together with lavender satin ribbons. "I wrote you letters, telling you how much I loved you and how proud I was of you. They kept me close to you."

She handed me the letters and said, "They're yours now". She softly kissed me on the forehead, tears trickling down my high cheekbones.

I came home prepared to forgive and realized there was nothing to forgive.

Our family has overcome tremendous challenges. We are strong, loving, resilient people. Yes, we have hurt each other on the journey, but none of us meant to cause harm.

It is all good and I am at peace.

I lay awake on the living room couch all night reading the letters.

"Adam, Aaron, Abel and Amos are all doing well. Adam is married with two children, living in Nigeria. He founded Ashur Homes in memory of our brother, a safe haven for urban youth seeking to get out of gangs and start a new life. The homes have spread to Chicago, Gary, Detroit, Los Angeles, and Las Vegas and expose youth to African cultural traditions such as oral history, storytelling, community, and rites of passage which is very healing to youth."

I felt happy after reading her letters.

Aaron graduated from Morehouse College and is an attorney in Atlanta. Abel and Amos travel frequently to help run the Ashur Homes. Mom saved their lives when she sent them home to Mother Africa.

Late that night I knock on my parent's bedroom door, careful not to wake my siblings. "May I come in?" I ask.

"Come in Sweetie," Momma whispers.

I climb into bed with my parents and it's as if the last 23

years never happened. I am a five-year-old girl.

Bliss.

I tell my parents the story of my mission, careful to be as believable as possible, so I leave out my powers.

"I always admired your strength and courage, Ashira, but this is too dangerous", Momma whispers.

"I am protected", I reply.

"How can we help you princess?" Dad interjects.

"You are already helping when mom's strength, love and dedication to her family grows and spreads to everyone around her. And when you share the gifts of art and music with youth and the community, you are making the world a brighter place. You both found happiness. You are helping." I reply.

"There is one other thing. We need all of you to travel to Nigeria with Ahmed, his family and Bilal. You will be safer there."

Dad and mom embrace me, as their love and strengthen envelop me.

"You got it", Dad reassures. "We can stay in one of Adam's Ashur Homes."

My Ancestors Are Here

In the limousine on the ride to the Four Seasons where Ahmed, his family and Bilal are waiting for me, I am still comforted by my parents' embrace as I mentally prepare for the incredible journey ahead. I lay alone on the crisp, soft, white sheets feeling great peace despite the danger.

I close my eyes.

The goddesses and Great-grandmother Katherine are around me. I recognize the beautiful water goddesses from my dreams after Ashur's death.

Mami Wata.

"You are never alone".

I feel Mother Goddess Asherah smiling.

"Love is the most powerful force in the universe. You are now pure love. Nothing can stop you. These are your instructions. You must do this on your own. Tell no one, but remember we are always with you, so you are never alone. You are a fierce Warrior Goddess. You and your army will conquer capitalism. Money and power will no longer be valued over life. Love is greater than capitalism. The root of capitalism is division. Like Israel, Africa was divided and conquered by capitalism. When Africa becomes united again, the world will know peace because Africa is the birthplace of civilization."

Mother Asherah continues, "You and Malcolm must come together as one as it was in the beginning. When you make love, the reunification of male and female will be sealed in the spiritual and physical worlds. This love will send a powerful beam of light which will pierce through this dimension and allow light from higher dimensions into Earth. This powerful light will realign the planets and awaken the gods and goddesses who are here to uplift Earth. The healing will begin."

Mother Asherah continues, "There will be a new Earth. Government will be run by people sharing power. There will be no more hierarchies. Everyone will be treated equal and live from the heart, so there will be no need for police or military. Wealth will be distributed and shared evenly. The truth will be revealed. This world has become a world of illusion, ruled by deception. Profit has become the foundation of every institution of today. Religion, education, government, justice, commerce, medicine, media. All these institutions must return to the foundation of love and care for all life. Failure is not an option, Ashira. If you fail, the Earth will be destroyed again."

Ashur appears in my dream later that night. He is standing at the stove making candy with butter and sugar.

He smiles at me.

"Sorry lil Sis. My soul has been resting, but I'm here now."

Like old times.

I'm so happy to see my brother. He came to me in dreams when he first died, but I haven't dreamed of him in years.

I love you Ashur.

"Just call when you need me lil Sis. I'll fight by your side. You're so loving you can't kill anyone, but I can. Don't be afraid", he whispers in my ear, hugging me tightly.

"I am not afraid." I reply confidently.

The flight to Peru is very long yet passes in minutes. I am preoccupied with my mission. Upon arrival in Puno, Peru I meet a group of goddesses on the same quest.

Jenna, a Dominican from New York comes to me and asks my birth date. *July 11th,* I reply. "So is mine!"

711, I think to myself.

I remember.

The date Tariq and Umm Hakim captured Spain and restored harmony.

I am on the right path.

Jenna and I become instant friends.

The Peruvians on the floating island of Uros are pleasant and friendly. They don't have a lot of material possessions, yet they are happy.

On the boat ride to the Andes our tour guide tells the folklore of Lake Titicaca. Puno is the folklore capitol of Peru. I am reminded of African folklore.

Greek mythology and Bible stories all come from African folklore.

As I am standing on the shore of Lake Titicaca the wind suddenly blows fiercely. A wave crashes onto the shore and grabs me into the water. The waves carry me out into the Lake and gently returns me to the shore. Yemoja and Mami Wata are all around. Purging me. Filling me. Machu Picchu is breathtaking. The sky and water are vibrant blue, and the air is so clear and pristine.

Pure.

The black mountains capped with white snow, majestic eagles. We climb to the top of Machu Picchu together. The mountains are so high that we can touch the clouds.

I eat cocoa leaves to keep oxygen supplied to my lungs. The air is thin at this altitude.

My ancestors were here.

In the sun temple we join hands, sitting in a circle in lotus position. Miraculously, I call on Esu, in Yoruba, an ancient Nigerian language that I never learned, to open the portal between the spiritual and physical worlds.

"Akọkọ ti o ṣe alalawọ Opener of

Ways,

Oluṣọ ti Crossroads, Oluwa ti o

yan,

Trickster ati Olùkọ, Imọlẹ ati

Ọlọgbọn Kan,

Jọwọ ṣe amọna mi lori ọna mi.

Mu mi lọ si oye, ati kuro ninu

ibi.

Fi han mi awọn asiri ti ara mi ati

ni agbaye ti o wa ni ayika

mi.

Ran mi lọwọ lati ranti iye ti

aifọwọyi ati asonu.

Fi awọn angẹli pupọ han mi, ọpọlọpọ awọn eroye ti o wa ni ayika gbogbo awọn ipo, Red ati Black, ki emi ki o le yan pẹlu ohun idaniloju ati ki o fun ni oye.

Alàgbà ati ọmọde,

Ẹlẹda,

Ẹlẹmi-mimu, Olukọni, iwọ ti a npe ni Esu, Eshu, Eleggua, Papa Legba,

Mo yìn ati kọrin si ọ.

Jowo ṣii ilẹkun.

Gba awọn adura mi, ki o si gbe wọn kọja awọn ọna arin."

"First honored Opener of the Ways,

Guardian of the Crossroads,

Lord of Choice,

Trickster and Teacher, Hermit and

Handsome One,

Please guide me upon my road.

Lead me into understanding and away

from evil.

Reveal to me the secrets in myself

and in the world around me.

Help me remember the value of

the overlooked and discarded.

Show me the many angles, the

many perceptions surrounding all

situations, the Red and Black, so

that I may choose with an agile

and informed mind.

Elder and child, Mischiefmaker,

Rum-drinker, Communicator, you who

are called Esu, Eshu,

Eleggua, Papa Legba,

I honor and sing to you.

Please open the gate.

Accept my prayers, and carry them

beyond the crossroads."

Suddenly Esu appears.

"The gate will open when you are

ready, Ashira."

12:12

I feel dread.

An evil presence surrounds me.

What is this?

I close my eyes and Ahmed's partner's face appears.

He is trying to find us!

I step off the plane looking around for signs of danger. A man grabs me from behind and says, "Do as I say, or you will die." Cold, hard metal pierces my lower back.

"Now walk toward the black limo and get inside". Ahmed's partner is in the car. He has on sunglasses to avoid my gaze. He punches me. The force knocks my head into the black leather seat. He puts his hands around my neck.

The air leaves my body as I lose consciousness.

I wake up lying naked on a bed. I am blind-folded, and my feet and hands are tied. "I will sell you for a lot of money Ashira, but first we must take care of one little thing." A goon takes the blindfold off.

"It's a shame, those eyes are so beautiful", Ahmed's partner sneers. The goon pushes his large thumbs into my eye sockets.

"Help me Ashur!" I scream.

Immediately Ashur appears.

He grabs the goon and throws him against the wall, killing him instantly. My ruby encrusted sword appears in my hand and Ashur and I fight off the rest of the goons.

Ahmed's partner flees undetected.

I must get to the Great Pyramid.

It's 11:00 am. Malcolm and I must reunite at exactly 12:12 pm. There is not much time. I call on the goddesses to place a force field around us so that Ahmed's partner cannot detect us.

The Warrior Goddesses surround us.

At first, I wondered why the Kings Chamber at the top of The Great Pyramid was chosen for our union, but as I stand in front of one of the Seven Wonders of the World, I am in awe. The Great Pyramid is the most amazing thing I have ever seen.

This massive structure built with the bare hands of skilled workers reminds me of the superhuman power of the Egyptians. Like the Egyptians, the Inca Indians of Peru were great architects.

The Kings Chamber of The Great Pyramid looks a lot like the sun temple at Machu Picchu. It is massive and is made entirely of pink granite.

The sides are constructed from limestone and granite and ceilings with pink granite. Within the chamber lies a red granite sarcophagus.

I climb to the top of the stairs, out of breath until I see my beloved Malcolm in the doorway. I feel relieved and relax at the sight of the man I adore.

We embrace.

Our bodies become one as we kiss. Malcolm gently lays me on the pallet lying next to the sarcophagus, and lovingly removes my long, white flowing dress. He looks into my eyes, kisses my lips, neck, and breasts so softly with his velvet lips.

He turns me on my stomach and softly runs his fingertips from the nape of my neck down my spine. I close my eyes, shivering in ecstasy. He sits up and crosses his legs in lotus position with his eyes fixed on my eyes.

I roll over and sit on his lap, wrapping my long legs around his toned body. He pulls me into him, and we kiss passionately. As we make love, Mother Asherah, Osun and the fertility goddesses dance around an Asherah Pole and perform the Nigerian Money Dance ritual to bless our union.

Our love making is like nothing I ever experienced with Ahmed. I feel as if my entire being is breathing in new life. Time stands still as we climax together; a bright beautiful light envelops us. I can feel our DNA intertwine as two become one.

Malcolm and I fall into a deep sleep. When we awaken, I feel tingling all over my body as the union becomes permanent.

Our next destination is Lagos, Nigeria. Adam has arranged for Baba to meet me there to assist with my initiation. Baba, a Yoruba Babalawo and seven female and male elders also participate in the nine-day initiation process.

I feel so loved and protected by all of them. The minute I stepped on African soil; I felt the powerful energy there. Before the initiation process began, we feasted on jollof rice, collard greens, fufu, plantains, and hibiscus lemonade.

The table was pread with all kinds of beautiful exotic fruit. Mango, watermelon, papaya, coconut.

All-natural and packed with nutrients.

The way we were meant to eat.

After the feast we danced. The beat of the drums and the chants possess me as I dance around in my beautiful skirt of nine colors.

I feel Oya take over my movements, like the Holy Ghost did Sister Partridge from back home. I wonder which Orisha was with her.

I cannot go into details of the initiation, but when I became filled with the spirit of Oya, I felt so much power surge through my body that I fell to the ground. I could hardly contain it.

The winds blew fiercely, and I could hear Oya's spirit directing me to call on the winds and tornadoes whenever I need them. When I arrive at the hotel and look in the bathroom mirror, I am amazed at my transformation.

I feel a warm glow as the tingling continues. The sensation is amazing. I feel high.

I fall into a deep sleep as the transformation and dramatic changes in my DNA continue.

While sleeping I have a sequence of dreams in which Harriet Tubman, Winnie Mandela and the Great African Queens speak to me about their victories. The Nubian Queens, Amanirenas, Shanakdakhete, Gudit, Amanitore, Amanishakheto, Amanitaraqide, Amanitu, Makeda of Sheba tell me their stories of great wealth and power. I was amazed at Queen Amanirenas' story of defeating Caesar Agustus. And with one eye!

If she could fight for five years until the Roman army retreated in defeat, I can win this fight.

The Egyptian Queens, Neferititi, Tiye, Hatshepsut; the Ethiopian Queens, Gudit, Empress Candace; the Nigerian Queen, Amina; the Ghanaian Queen, Yaa Asantewaa;

the Algerian Queen, Al-Kahina; the Madagascar Queen Ranavola; the Angolan Queen Nzinga; and the South African Queen Nandi all tell their stories.

Filling me with courage and strength.

I awaken a week later light-headed and nauseas. I drink plenty of water with fresh lemon as hives break out all over my face and body while the cleansing process takes place, a gushing river of toxins and negative energies are released into the toilet.

There is a tingling along my spine from my tailbone up to the nape of my neck, and it feels like it is stretching.

Growing.

My curvy body is now lean and athletic. My black, long curly locks are now short, tight, vibrant red coils. The hives clear up after three days, revealing new skin. My brown skin glistens as if covered in clear crystals.

I am ready.

Holding Malcolm's hand on the plane ride to Israel I reflect on what I've noticed since the transformation. I keep seeing the numbers 411, 414, 144 on clocks, in newspapers and on the internet.

What does it mean? 411 means information. What information am I missing?

Suddenly it comes to me. April 14. That's the date I met Malcolm. I Google April 14th and discover historical events on that day. It is the day of the Jewish Passover. I Google April 14, 2014. Not only is it the date of a total eclipse or blood moon, but it's also the date 276 Nigerian girls were abducted from school.

"Boko Haram kidnapped Nigerian schoolgirls likely facing forced labor, sexual assault" the headline reads.

"Girls who have escaped describe horrific experiences, including being beaten and threatened with death for refusing to convert to Islam. Other girls were forced into marriages with Boko Haram fighters, including a 17-year-old who objected that she was too young. Her captor pointed at his 5-year-old daughter and said she was married the previous year and was waiting for puberty for the marriage to be consummated".

How is human trafficking in Nigeria connected to Pakistan?

This is not Islam, for true Islam honors all.

The street gangs in Englewood are much like the armed Muslim forces of Prophet Muhammad who went on raids and massacred the Jewish tribes in Arabia. The men who refused to convert were beheaded—and women were forcibly converted and kept as wives or slaves. Boko Haram's behavior is typical of any group fighting for survival.

For power.

The forty-minute plane ride is too short to explore. Malcolm and I sit, holding hands, contemplating quietly the next step.

"We have friends on the Palestinian Legislative Council. They have scheduled a meeting with President Mahmoud Abbas and the former Prime Minister of Palestinian National Authority, Salam Fayyad upon our arrival in Israel", Malcolm whispers, looking lovingly into my eyes.

"The PLC has not met since 2007, so this is groundbreaking, My Love."

"How did Palestine and Israel split?" I question. "Palestine never split off from Israel. They are one. The fight is over land and resources", Malcolm replies. I nod my head in agreement, thinking of the Gangster Disciples in Englewood and Boko Haram in Nigeria. "If only they knew their true identity, they would not fight. We must awaken them!" I exclaim.

The meeting takes place in a building much like the office buildings in New York. Malcolm and I shake hands with President Mahmoud Abbas, and former Prime Minister Salam Fayyad. I can feel the goddesses in the room, invisible to the others.

"What needs to take place is a change of heart. A change of how we see ourselves and each other. All the boundaries and borders have separated us, blinded us to our connections. We all want the same things. Why not work together? Share. Mother Earth belongs to all, not one. This includes Israel. West Bank, Gaza and Israel are all one", I proclaim passionately.

Surprisingly, Abbas and Fayyad agree.

"All we are seeking is justice and equality", Abbas interjects. "President Rivlin seems sympathetic to our concerns. Let us meet with him."

"Run!" Malcolm yells, as we leave the building. He notices

a child standing in the middle of the street with a bomb strapped to his chest.

Abbas and Fayyad are whisked to safety by the bodyguards while Malcolm runs to free the child from the bomb. He cuts the bomb loose and runs down an alley away from the pedestrians scampering for cover.

The bomb detonates.

A cloud of grey smoke fills the air in the distance. I grab the child and run. Security forces run after us.

We run into a church nearby. It is dark, and we hide behind a wooden pew, hoping we are not

detected. I pray silently for Oya
to protect us as the sound of heavy
boots on the wooden floor gets
closer and closer.

Time stands still.

Holding my breath, eyes
closed, I hug the child close to
me.

The soldier drags us outside,
throwing us to the ground. The
soldier hits me in the face with the
butt of his rifle.

Where are you Oya?

I lose consciousness.

I wake up on the floor of a
jail cell. My face and body bloody
and bruised. Ahmed's partner is

sitting in a wooden chair looking down at me.

"You will not escape this time. Your love is not more powerful than me. I have forces working for me just like you do. They are everywhere. Your Malcolm is dead, so what will you do now?"

I lay there, listless. Too weak to call on Ashur.

Suddenly, Ahmed's partner and the soldiers guarding me fall to the ground, paralyzed. The door to the cell opens and Malcolm walks in.

"I will never leave you, My Love." He runs to me, pulls me into his arms, looks into my eyes and places his left hand gently on my belly and right hand on my heart. I feel the heat and am instantly healed.

I feel abandoned by the goddesses. I don't understand why they didn't protect us.

Immediately Oya speaks to me. "You don't need us anymore. You can command the wind and tornadoes, but also use the power of your words. Your ruby encrusted sword represents the power of words. The word combined with love is an unstoppable force. Use your power!"

In Jerusalem Malcolm and I meet with President Reuven Rivlin,

President Shimon Peres, former President of Israel, President Mahmoud Abbas, and former Prime Minister Salam Fayyad. We discuss the recent events that led to the current conflict, all related to money and the Ottoman Empire era.

President Reuven Rivlin narrates, "In the 1800s Europeans who converted to Judaism were relocated to Israel due to oppression in Germany. It was called the Zionist Movement. Judaism was adopted as a material basis for capitalism rather than religion. In 1901 The Jewish National Fund was founded at the

Fifth Zionist Congress in Basel with the aim of buying and developing land in the southern region of Ottoman Syria for Jewish settlement. In 1993 Bill Clinton, Yitzhak Rabin and Yasser Arafat signed the Oslo Accords. In 2002 as a result of the significant increase of suicide bombing attacks in Israel, the West Bank Fence along the Green Line border was constructed to protect Israeli civilians from Palestinian terrorism."

President Rivlin continues, "In 2005 evacuation of 25 Jewish settlements in the Gaza Strip and

West Bank was completed. In 2006 the Second Lebanon War took place. In 2009 a large-scale military operation in the Gaza Strip ensued. In 2012 Operation Pillar of Cloud launched a large-scale military operation in the Gaza Strip in response to Palestinian militants firing over a hundred rockets from the Gaza Strip into southern Israel, with the aims of restoring peace."

"You mentioned the Ottoman Empire", I interject. "What role does this era play in the current conflict?"

Former President Peres replies, "The Ottoman's are my

ancestors. The Ottoman Empire ruled from 1300-1923 and was a monarchy ruled by Sultans. They were the male dominated center of interactions between east and west for six centuries. Territories included Southeast Europe, Western Asia the Caucasus, border of Europe and Asia, Turkey and the Middle East. The Empire became a melting pot that absorbed cultures and ended the free-flowing commerce of artisans, merchants and agriculturalists. The Ottoman elite established a society with religion as a foundation for slavery. Female slaves were sold as late as 1908.

There were Imperial harems. Eunuchs were castrated without consent and forced to become harem servants. The Empire dissolved after World War I."

The Ottoman Empire sex slavery reminds me of Boko Haram. "How do we end this madness? Human beings are not property. All life has equal value", I proclaim. "Sex slavery has spread globally, in Nigeria, Pakistan, the US. Everywhere. In this quest for peace, we must end sex slavery."

"Yes, Ashira", former Prime Minister Salam Fayyad replies. "Harems and sex slavery are intertwined in Middle Eastern culture. Women and children are viewed as property."

"Most cultures view some part of the population as property. We must open our eyes and evolve. Women and men are equal!" I proclaim passionately.

"We will meet with the United Nations next." Malcolm interjects.

Love Heals

That night in the hotel while meditating, I call on my ancestor Tariq.

Guide me to the truth.

"I've been waiting for you to call me Ashira!" Tariq proclaims.

"How is all this connected Tariq?" I inquire.

"The Arabian Peninsula was not good for agriculture and there were just a few towns and cities; Mecca and Medina were two of them. Agriculture thrived in Medina, while Mecca was the financial center for many surrounding tribes.

Communal life was essential for survival in the desert conditions."

Tariq continues, "politically, Arabia at the time was divided between two tribes, the Banu Qais and Banu Kalb from Yemen, allies with Sassanid Persia. These rivalries were suppressed by Islam but continued to influence the Middle East and North Africa before Islam. Prophet Muhammad was a Hanif and one of the descendants of Ishmael, son of Abraham. Hanifs had beliefs similar to Jews and Christians. Boko Haram is behaving like the armed Muslim force from Muhammad's time. The Prophet's warriors went on raids and massacred the Jewish tribes in Arabia. The men who refused to convert were beheaded and then the Prophet divided the women, children, houses, and chattels among the Muslims. The women were forced to convert to Islam and kept as wives or slaves."

Take me to the Boko Haram leader.

I immediately feel connected to Abubakar Shekau. I feel his heart.

This man has heart, much like the street gang leaders in Englewood seeking voice, belonging, power and basic needs where they could find it.

"Speak to his heart, Ashira. Everyone has a heart, no matter how evil they seem. No one is evil at heart. Light is the only transforming force. Where there is no light, there is the potential for transformation, nothing else. The truth has been hidden. We have judged and divided, now it is time to bring the light everywhere, Ashira. Bring the light to Abubakar Shekau. The number 144 signals light. Awaken the light in him. Shine the light wherever it is absent when you see this number." Tariq whispers. "Hear him. He is no more fanatical than anyone else who holds strongly to religious beliefs."

I remain connected to Abubakar's heart and ask him to tell his story. You are a brilliant and powerful man, though misguided. When you hurt those girls, you hurt yourself. They are a part of you. They are that part of you that is loving, kind, creative. Why have you rejected those parts of yourself?"

"I too was hurt. When I was a child the Nigerian police killed my family. I was an orphan, growing up on the street. I just wanted to do something to show the world how

great I am. I am smart. I am good."
Nodding, I reply. "Yes, you are.
Now you have the power to restore
peace in Nigeria. The Nigerian
military has oppressed you. I
understand your anger. This is not
the way. Return the girls to their
families and ask forgiveness."

"But I will be killed",
Abubukar counters. "Yes, but your
soul will rest, knowing you
fulfilled your mission. Returning
those precious girls is a powerful
act of love that will touch many.
You can help us reunite all as one
again. All religions can coexist
peacefully. There is no need to

force others to believe what you believe."

I remind him of the warrior Tariq's mission of peace and tolerance.

"You have the attention of the world. They see you as a terrorist. Show them who you really are. You can help finish what Tariq started. Instead of just Spain, let's spread it across the globe."

"I am with you, Ashira. Thank you for enlightening me, my dear sister", Abubakar replies as peace covers his face.

His appearance changes instantly as the light awakens in

him. I see the light surrounding him. I smile. I wake up from deep meditation and snuggle into Malcolm.

I use my powers to intercept programming at CNN, MSNBC and Fox who simultaneously broadcast live globally, Abubakar telling where the girls are, revealing the heads of human trafficking in every nation, including Pakistan.

He reveals key figures globally involved in the sex trade, including Jeffrey Epstein and many other influential people in America.

Then, I speak.

"America uses media to control minds globally. The internet and social media have opened the world to power and money hungry people who seek to control its wealth and resources. People willingly give up their power now."

"Chains are no longer necessary." I continue fearlessly.

"People can be influenced to do anything that is put in their face on Facebook, YouTube and Instagram. And now the world's wealth and resources are controlled by America. The new Ottoman Empire. People migrate to America to escape poverty. Breaking up families, sacrificing spirit, culture. And for what? Money? Most are still poor and powerless. The truth has been hidden for centuries and has come to light. Children are the bearers of the truth. They have been bought and sold as property, overlooked, abused. No more!"

Malcolm and I return to the United States to a hero's welcome. The $7 million-dollar reward offered by the United States is given to me and my army of children who serve humanity by bringing the light to Earth. A Children's Fund is established for girls and boys affected by human trafficking. In a press conference at the White House, President Obama addresses the nation about our heroic efforts.

"Ashira and her army have shown that children will no longer be overlooked, disregarded and pushed away. These children are part of a new race coming to Earth. It is time for men, women and children to come together as one. Listen to each other, learn from each other, embrace and empower each other. You are each other. The awakening has begun."

In a United Nations meeting the following week I announce to global leaders as Malcolm looks at me adoringly, his eyes sparkling.

"Thank you for gathering here today. Each of you is in power now because of your heart. It is time for us to revolve as human beings. To get back to who we were in Africa when humanity was born. Lay down your weapons and share this planet. There is enough abundance on Earth for everyone to share. We must return to nature, to our true selves. In seven years, the transformation will be complete. Balance will be restored to Earth. It is up to each of us to right the wrongs of our ancestors. We have

come   full   circle.   Let   the
revolution be complete. Open your
heart to love and let the light in.
Those who refuse will be purged."

The next morning Malcolm and I
return to Nigeria where we are
taught by the Elders hidden wisdom
about our original way of life when
we were one. Family and community
were everything and everyone lived
together, peacefully, in love and
harmony.

We learn about Olodumare, the
Creator God who is female and male.
We also learn about the great West
African empires, Mali, Songhai and

Timbuktu with its streets paved with gold.

I meditate on Oya, Yemoja, Osun, Mami Wata, and Asherah to receive power and guidance for seven days. On the seventh day Esu appears and opens the portal between the spiritual and physical worlds.

I call the winds and fire to purge the Earth.

Oya and her mate Sango along with the Warrior Goddesses appear. Immediately tornadoes, thunderstorms, and fires spread across the planet.

I call the water to purge the Earth.

Yemoja and her mate Olokun appear with Mami Wata. Immediately hurricanes, tsunamis, earthquakes, and volcano eruptions spread across the planet.

The natural disasters descend upon the Earth so rapidly and forcefully that no one can prepare for or run from them. In thirty days all violent, greedy, negative energies on Earth are purged for the New Earth to emerge.

Africa is the only continent untouched by the natural disasters. On the thirtieth day I call on Osun and her mate, Ogun, the Iron Maker. They seal the Earth with the strength and power of love, so that no one and nothing can ever destroy it again.

The 144,000 awakened gods and goddesses who migrated to Africa are the lone survivors and are reunited with their soul mates. In seven years, balance is restored. Together we rebuild the New Earth where creation started. As it was in the beginning.

Ashira's World.

THE END

Divine Love Poem
By Alicia Nunn

My man is Beautiful

Like rays of sunlight his smile

illuminates the depths of my soul

As he looks into me with those

eyes.

Those eyes are kindly and gently

unfolding me

As they see me, not just this sexy

frame I'm in, but into me

Like an ancient script he reads me

He knows my Spirit

That part of me that is endless and

free

He embraces me

With his caresses he blesses

Every day he amazes me.

My man is Strong

His strength empowers me

You see he's not ripped with

muscles He doesn't tussle or

hustle for power, no he uplifts me

With his unconditional love and

acceptance of me

He does not seek to own or possess

me. He releases me

To be free

He understands me.

My man is Wise

The wisdom of generations of

Africans flows through his DNA And

as I lay in his arms, I feel the

knowledge of the ages enter me

Through his energy

My ancestors reveal to me

All that we are meant to be.

The male and female energy

Together

Finally

You see he is me and I am he.

Like a mirror he reflects to me

Our destiny

Divinity

Twin flames, sacred energy Of the

same soul once divided now one

again Whole again

Unity.

CPSIA information can be obtained
at www.ICGtesting.com
Printed in the USA
BVHW071327180521
607630BV00004B/273